WHEN

I SAY

JUMP!

BY

Gibran Tariq

ACKNOWLEDGMENTS

Without preamble, I bear witness that there is no God but Allah and that He alone is worthy of worship.

I, as always, thank my beloved family members. They have offered me unfailing support over the years and without their love and support, I would have perished emotionally a long time ago. Thanks, family, for being there. What's up, Aaliyah?

I also give a shout to my FB family who keep me inspired and encouraged. Peace. I would also like to thank Brotha Troy Johnson at AALBC who befriended me when I was still in prison and offered me some invaluable advice which he is still doing nowadays.

I give props to the brothers and sisters who labor inside the belly of the beast, especially the ones with whom I have broken bread, or walked the yard, or gone to war with. Martin Petty from Greensboro, NC. Man, I pray all is well with you. I could always count on you. The same goes for Willie Dick, my first partner inside the Youth Center back in the days. Oh yeah, Big Bam, (Frank Goodman), I know I have said it before but I SENT THAT MONEY. Eli "Big E" Easterling. Where are you brotha? Holla! Forrest "PeeWee" Malker. I know you short, my brotha. Praise Yah!

I have spent 35 years in some of the toughest prisons in the country and have met some of the best people in the world.

I NOW PROUDLY PROCLAIM THAT I AM A LION FROM THE TRIBE OF JUDAH!!!

BOOK I

She had done it!

When Elizabeth Sellers had graduated from Howard University, she thought she would have to hire a personal secretary just to field all the urgent phone calls and emails she would be receiving from prominent law firms across the country as they tried to lure her into their private practice. And why not? She was bright, beautiful, and dynamic. Qualities that would wear well under anyone's shingle, but they would have to act fast since it was her intention to enter into her own practice after a few years.

Here I am she challenged the world. Are you ready for me, the beautiful, black female equivalent of Johnny Cochran?

She had had it all planned out. First, she would conquer New York, dazzling the legal world of Gotham City with her fresh, brilliant strategies and once she had made her first few million dollars in corporate law, she would return to Washington to practice criminal law.

Without so much as a second thought, she had fled the college scene and had spent what money she had in renting a fashionable address and buying law books. She had also bought three phones because she didn't want to miss any of the important calls once they started pouring in. During those dreamy, heady months, she had been delirious with anticipation, but no calls ever came. *Reality did.* It had taken some doing but it had finally gotten through to her that great grades on the LSAT were not negotiable instruments with any real value in the real world.

From the billing period of August through September, a disturbing pattern emerged. No calls had come in from any law firms--- large or small. No calls. No messages. Nothing.

By summer's end, she had been forced to abandon her "address of substance" for a street level apartment in Northeast DC. She had adopted a cat and for the very first time in her life, she appropriately felt that she was unable to help herself. She had never been overly religious and while she felt it would be hypocritical to beg for divine assistance, she did. She thanked God that her needs were not so great.

By denying herself all but the minimum required to survive, she would eke out an existence, but one night before crying herself to sleep, she absently wondered how would any law firm know where she was. The phones---all three of them---were off.

Despite all her adversity, she had prevailed. From some Muslim friends, she had learned how to fast, consuming nothing during the daylight hours. With her stomach sufficiently shrunken, feeding herself would be less expensive.

She didn't wait for the authorities to shut off the lights in her apartment. She had pride. She turned them off herself, plunging her world into a darkness that was a perfect match for the blackness that consumed her soul.

Things continued to get worse.

On her way to and from her personal errands, she noticed how oblivious the entire world was to what was happening to her, and other than the heavily-religious encouragement from her mother, there were no other public cries of support. No band. No cheering section. Nothing. She was alone and whenever she caught a glimpse of herself as she strolled past a picture glass window on some sparkling government building that is exactly how she looked. *Alone.*

Elizabeth fondly remembered the day, years earlier, when she had enrolled at Howard. She remembered that initially, she had wanted to attend UCLA, but at the last possible moment had opted instead to study in the nation's capital. She had decided it would never be too early to establish a personal relationship with the city she intended to have eating out of her hands. In DC, the stuffy bureaucracy and the law were always churning, setting the legal trends for the rest of the country. Washington was Rome. All roads led there and she had wanted a head start.

Each day during those times when her workload had permitted, she would browse the Library of Congress, looking, peering, and learning. She would visit all the haunts of the city's power brokers and if by chance she spotted or recognized someone whom she deemed worthy of her emulation, she would stand in the exact spot where he or she had stood, mentally infusing herself with their power. Pretty soon, she had kiddingly come to view herself as a political vampire. When she spied a victim, she had no desire to suck their neck. She'd rather bite into their skull and drain them of every drop of their power. And she'd still want more.

Almost every day, this had been her habit; to go hunting, mentally sucking the power out of every politician, corrupt or otherwise, that she saw. Now, years later, she felt as powerless as a newborn infant.

Then she got a letter in the mail.

Nowadays, Elizabeth, a slender, light-skinned woman with soft brown eyes, frizzy hair, and long legs, was a legal dynamo. She had returned to her hometown, Charlotte, and had joined the legal firm of Truman, Daniels, Thornton, and Bailey. She had immediately set the place on its ear. She attacked the office files and gently scolded the senior partners for letting so many bread and butter cases languish in the musty old file cabinets. She plucked up case after case, breathing new legal vitality into them and taking them to court. Time after time, she settled, very rarely with any resistance. Only once did she have to go to trial. Her reputation spread.

It was around this time that a case came to her attention.

One morning, a Friday in early October, a very pretty, very young, black woman was in the office, speaking with the secretary. As soon as she entered, the secretary waved her over and whispered. "I think you should speak with this young lady."

Elizabeth politely escorted the woman, Deborah Hill, back to her office, who then explained how her youngest son, Warren and another boy, both three years old, had been struck by an automobile while at day care.

Being left unattended, the boys had wandered off together and had tried to cross the street. It had been noon, the exact time when that particular Charlotte Street was busy with lunchtime traffic. Both boys were struck by a passing car. They were rushed to Carolinas Medical Center and when the police had arrived to conduct an investigation, no one on the scene had had any idea who the children were. When one of the officers had decided to inquire at the day care, the lone woman in charge had indicated to the officer that all her children were well and accounted for. She told the officer that it was tragic that kids were not more closely supervised.

Both of the boys had been listed in critical condition initially, but later their conditions were stabilized.

When Miss Hill had returned that evening to pick up her son, she noticed another young woman standing outside the reception area, weeping. She had politely asked if she was okay and if there was anything she could do for the woman. The woman said no and continued to cry. Miss Hill had then entered the receptionist's office and signed her son out. Then it became apparent to her that something was wrong when Warren had not come running to greet her. She had glared at the supervisor, but before she could ask where her son was, two police came through the play area.

"Are you Miss Hill?" one of them had inquired.

When she had affirmed that she indeed was Deborah Hill, the CMPD officer had mournfully informed her that her son was missing and that they had combed every inch of the premises and were absolutely convinced that he was not there.

Deborah Hill explained that it wasn't until the evening news that she and the other woman, Tamara Sloan, had found out precisely where their sons were. Thank God for Channel 14 News.

Deborah Hill went on to explain that she wanted to have the best lawyer available. So did Miss Sloan. And they both wanted her. Would she be interested? There was no question about the merits of the case Deborah assured her and Elizabeth readily agreed. Safety Pins Day Care Center was decidedly negligent and was, as a result, liable.

Elizabeth also knew that most clients sought swift, irrevocable justice or compensation, especially when they felt they had a good case. She likewise recognized that any unnecessary delays could place a great deal of strain on lawyer-client relationships and knew that the opposing team would plug away at their resistance by begging the state for delays. To combat this strategy, an option would be to place the case squarely in the lap of a federal judge. Even though she had never been inside a federal courtroom, Elizabeth knew that this might be the way to pursue this matter----if she decided to handle the case.

"Is there anything else about this case I should be made aware of?" Elizabeth asked.

"That's it as far as Miss Sloan and I are concerned."

"You think there are other issues involved?"

"Well, I know for a fact that one boy at Safety Pins almost drowned during the summer, and Miss Sloan said she knew of a mother whose son had fallen out of the high chair and had to be hospitalized. There's probably more. Nobody has ever investigated."

Elizabeth wanted to commit right away, but she didn't need a crusade. And Deborah Hill and Tamara Sloan didn't need a crusader. They needed a lawyer.

"Let me check on a few things," Elizabeth offered, "and you can call me on Tuesday. I'll have an answer for you then."

When the office was clear, Elizabeth took her phone off the hook and told the secretary to field all her messages. For some reason, she felt the unbearable torment of hell fixing to break loose. She believed that if she opened this can of worms that it would turn out to be Pandora's Box.

On the Wednesday before Halloween, Elizabeth arranged to meet with the four families involved in The Safety Pins Day Care Center case. She had decided to include the cases of the other two boys injured at Safety Pins to bolster her show of gross negligence. When the women, all black, arrived in her office they appeared suspicious. Only Deborah Hill seemed relaxed and focused. The other women may have suspected that all Elizabeth saw was the chance to make a quick buck and therefore would attempt to influence them to take the money and run without putting any real pressure on Safety Pins. More than anything else, the women had all agreed that they wanted the facility shut down. Forever. Always. Permanently.

Once the introductions were formally dispensed with, the four women stared helplessly at Elizabeth who dutifully expounded upon the pros and cons of a case like the one they wished to pursue against Safety Pins. She gave them examples of how long it sometimes took to develop a case even though the injury and neglect were visible and apparent, pointing out that delays and countermeasures could keep a case away from resolution for years at a time, causing a loss of interest on the plaintiff's part.

Without hesitation she aptly described how lax state regulatory laws allowed duly licensed facilities to operate despite serious violations. The faces of the women registered worry when she outlined the amount of money her firm would have to invest in order to effectively fight the case.

"I don't wish to sound indifferent to your struggle," Elizabeth informed the women, "but I have to be honest. I understand perfectly that each of you has had sons injured, almost killed by this place and I know that right now revenge is as good a motive as any to want to sue the pants off of Safety Pins. I can deal with that. No problem. I understand. Now, what I must persuade each of you to understand is that my attachment to this case may appear entirely different. Yes, I wish to see justice served in this particular situation and I'll fight to see that it is, but I also must work on behalf of my firm. I must be concerned that my firm doesn't lose money or go broke fighting this case." She waited for a response. "Do you understand?"

Regina Taylor, an attractive, light-skinned woman with short, blond-colored hair answered. "It means that you can take the case and not give a damn about us or our children just as long as your boss, Mr. Charlie, gets his paper back."

Elizabeth's mood was somber. "Actually, that's an exaggeration I could protest, but it could be partially true. Law is a business and I very well could take this case and not give a shit about anything other than the profit ratio, but that's not true. I'm a black woman and I sincerely and deeply care about what happens to us. I'm not some lucky bitch from across the tracks. I'm from the hood and when you look at it realistically, we've got to stick together. Those may be your sons, but they represent the future of black people everywhere and if I'm in a position to help, I shouldn't resist. It just may be that one of your sons may be the next Malcolm or Martin and Lord knows, we are going to need them the ways things are going in this country." Elizabeth paused. "Are we down or what?"

The women all smiled. *Sistas.* They were down.

"Good." Elizabeth seemed pleased that she was accepted. "Now let's get down to business."

The conversation started with Angie Cummings, a short, dark woman with luminous eyes. She had dropped her son, Lothario, off at the day care and had gone on to work. Just before she was to leave on her lunch break, she had been notified that there was an emergency phone call on hold for her at the company's office. Rushing to the office, she learned that the call had been made by the Director of Safety Pins. Miss

Cummings had calmly been informed that her son had toppled from his high chair and that she should hurry over to Carolinas Medical to check on his condition.

Elizabeth listened attentively. She took notes.

Regina Taylor's story was next. Her son, Vincent, had slipped through the open gate at the deserted swimming pool and within minutes was found floating face down in the blue water, unconscious. Fortunately, another mother who left her child at Safety Pins on a part-time basis spotted the child and pulled him out of the pool. Fortunately, the paramedics, when they arrived, were able to revive Vincent who, as a result, did suffer some brain and tissue damage.

In the end, Elizabeth sighed. "It's not going to be easy for them to justify negligence of this magnitude," she admitted. "One thing for certain is that Safety Pins can't adopt a cheery mistakes-do-sometimes-happen approach to this case. That much is certain." She looked over her notes. "God knows, they incompetent."
"So you think we can win?" Regina inquired.

Elizabeth leaned back, pondering her strategy. She confessed. "I've done some snooping and they have hired a very good attorney. He is flamboyant and thrives on good theater. He uses the courtroom as a stage, but," she mused, "I don't think that even Hilton Jenners III would want to go to trial on this one." She traded high fives with the women. "I think we got them by the balls."

As soon as he got the case in his hands, Hilton Jenners III, a gracefully-aging, blond male with a silver moustache, made contact. He didn't hesitate.

"And just what do you expect me to do down in Dixie with this piece of shit? I wouldn't want to go to trial with this case even if the plaintiff had Peter Griffin from Family Guy as their counsel." He crossed and uncrossed his long legs.

"Hold on, old buddy and get a grip. I trust you'll do what has to be done to get us out of the jungle in one piece." Senator Gaylord spoke calmly. "We'll concede to a consent decree, promising to clean up our act if the center is allowed to remain open. There's plenty riding on this one and we cannot afford to get shut down because it's our intention to expand the Safety Pins brand nationally."

Jenners laughed. "You're going to have to forgive me from finding this amusing, but given Safety Pins' track record, that would be like exporting a virus across the country. Those people down there are morons."

"Go ahead," the Senator challenged," kick me in the teeth, but those were not my people. All the freaking mishaps, every frigging one of them, happened when none of my people were there. Anyway, have you run a background check on the bimbo the plaintiffs hired?"

"No," Jenners admitted. "What's her story?"

""Bitch is still wet behind the ears. Been in trial only once. That's it."

"If she's that green, why didn't you just scare her off the case?"

"Why, and deprive you, you ol' devil, of giving her a premature bout of menopause."

"Jenners sighed. "I'll see what I can do. And please don't do me any more favors."

"Goodbye Paladin"

Paladin.

For the last fourteen years, that's what he had been for Senator Gaylord. A Paladin. A legal hit-man riding the fence for the big money interests of the high and mighty. It put food on the table and kept his Ferrari gassed up. No complaints there.

He had met Junius Gaylord in college. UCLA. Both had graduated summa cum laude with degrees in law, both choosing to practice on opposite coasts. Gaylord had made a name for himself in DC while he had remained in California. As the personal computer industry had blossomed and mushroomed under the nurturing sun of California North, Jenners had found himself a tiny space in a tiny office park and had hung out his shingle.

Back then he was simply another lawyer. Back then he chose cases he could believe in, whose merits he trusted. Back then, it was fun slaying the dragons, but it wasn't always like that when he worked for his old college chum, Junius Gaylord. In those cases, he usually was the dragon. In those cases, the dragon usually won.

It had all began with congratulations.

After a really exhausting, highly publicized legal shootout with a software company and its blatantly anticompetitive practices, he had hardly sat down to savor the victory than he had received a hastily scrawled note on white parchment. It had been from Gaylord.

"KUDOS!"

Starting at that moment, no matter what courtroom, no matter what city, he could always sense the invisible presence of Junius Gaylord, peering over his shoulder. It was almost like his friend was following him, zealously stalking him.

Immediately after winning a technically demanding royalty payment in Texas.

"KUDOS!"

In Wichita, Kansas.

"KUDOS!"

Junius Gaylord seemed to be everywhere at once.

2

The mahogany conference table was set into a rotunda. The room was well-lit and spacious; the soft, grey carpet, thick and plush. Gigantic, arched windows that were squeaky clean, cast a clear view of the panorama below.

At nine o'clock prompt, the men seated around the table ceased talking and Senator Junius Gaylord stepped forward as if this quietude, this act of obeisance, was his cue. He cleared his throat. The men fidgeted.

Junius Gaylord who acted as if he was larger than life was actually only 5'5" tall. His belly which hung over his belt made him look even shorter. His mouth was a cruel twist of flesh, but his blue eyes forever sparkled.

"We're in this for the money, gentlemen," he said reproachfully, "so there is no need for a speech." He paused. "However, I'd like to play with some figures."

His voice turned cold. A silent moment before he could say anything else, there was a brief knock on the door. The Senator guardedly nodded at Lemon, awarding him the privilege of answering the door. It was an orderly with a small portable laser projector. "Sit it on the table. Thanks."

The Senator phoned his secretary and directed her to hold all his calls, explaining gruffly that he didn't want to be disturbed under any circumstances. Immediately, a foreboding sense of suspense suffused the room, riveting each man's attention to the projector. The lights dimmed. Anticipation was rabid. The Senator spoke through the darkness, his voice eerily disengaged and distant.

"Today, I will demonstrate the viability of my vision to establish a multi-billion enterprise based on goods that are inexhaustible." He snapped on the projector. It cast a dazzling red-blue haze of light against the back wall, and slowly, from a darkened corner, Senator Gaylord walked into the glare, using it as a spotlight. He became iridescent. "Before my presentation, I wish to provide you with some background data." He paused dramatically. *"I hate niggers!"*

None of the men present were bleeding heart liberals so not a single one flinched at the racist sentiment of the Senator. They mutely listened as he fleshed out the events of his early life, sharing deeply-held secrets with them. They all knew that today, the man standing before them was facing demons that had to be exposed.

The Senator's voice rang with conviction and fire. "I don't consider my hate racist. Too me, it's very rational." He sucked in air. "I don't despise them because they are black. I detest them because they are animals. As such they deserve to be locked away." He took in another mouthful of air. "When I was young, very young, they raped my mother. I saw the entire act---everything. I can still hear her screaming, pleading for mercy. I can still see her fighting, trying to resist." He swallowed. "They beat her. They raped her. They escaped justice."

He walked through the spectrum of light, shredding it until he reached the edge of the table. He leaned over it; his hands pressed stiff and flat upon the surface. His voice was as hard as nails. "I knew then that the best thing to do for a nigger was to lock him up. It was some time quite later that I figured out how to profit from this realization and since that moment, my friends, my vision has been a labor of love. And now, today, I invite each of you to participate fully. The dream can be obtained." He stood straight. "I know I have been purposely vague on the finer points of what I hope will become our shared goal, but now you will see the methods behind my push to lock the black animals up." He flicked the projector on. It hummed softly, briefly, and then threw up an image. "Gentlemen" the Senator said with a flourish. "Meet Eugene Larry!"

He froze the frame. Spiteful pride skewered across his face. He gloated. *"Behold the man!"* He stabbed the pointer at the image. The thrusts were vicious, hate-filled. "This is our prototype, our model for the rest of the niggers." He lowered his eyes reverently. "On the tenth anniversary of my dear mother's death, I commenced my historic experiment and as a memorial to the sanctity of my mother's memory, I adopted this nigger who was born on September 1st, 1962." Gaylord gasped at the ugly thought the men harbored. "By God, no, I didn't literally adopt the bastard. That would have been a sacrilege. What I did do on that rainy morning was to select him to test my pet theory. We, Mr. Larry and I, have never met, never spoken, but he has performed wonderfully."

Senator Gaylord poured himself a glass of water. Sipping slowly, he reached out and touched the face on the screen. "As mentioned, the nigger and I have never met but never has he been absent from my control. I have played the role of a puppeteer and unbeknownst to him, he has been a most marvelous puppet. Basically, I have engineered all the major decisions of his life, forcing him even against his better interests to do exactly as I have wanted him to do. I was one student who personalized the work of B.F. Skinner, Watson. And Pavlov. I took them to task for what they reputed in their legendary studies and to my utter delight found their methods scientifically workable. That's why today, I place such emphasis on research and development."

Alfred McManus was the first to speak. "Senator, sir," he began, "if we are to believe what you suggest, that would mean that you have, in some manner, studied behavioral modification---."

The Senator interrupted. "Not studied. *Practiced!* I practiced behavioral modification on Eugene Larry." He grinned. "And now you can do the same thing." He turned the projector off. "With my money and influence, I was to see to it that his family remained poor. I kept a sharp eye on his schooling, making sure he attended only substandard schools." He grinned. "No matter how brilliant a teacher is, if the proper resources and teaching tools are non-existent, then so are that teacher's skills. No matter how brilliant the student may be, if he goes to school hungry, how can he concentrate? My puppet was perpetually hungry. I saw to this. In say, 1975 or so, I decided it was time for the father to abandon the family."

"You mean you-----"

"I did exactly that, sir" Gaylord interjected. "I arranged for the mother to land a good-paying job working at a local company in Charlotte. Then mysteriously, the father lost his job." The Senator winked devilishly. "Soon, the fool felt emasculated and cheap. One day he left. That was the easy part. When Larry was eleven, I felt it was time to expose the theory to maximum risk. I wanted him to steal."

"And just how did you manage that feat?" Alfred McManus was curious.

"Simple," Senator Gaylord bragged. "Next door to him lived his best friends, three brothers. I had someone shop around at a police bicycle auction and buy four bikes. Three of these bikes were immaculate. They had horns, lights, and reflectors, chrome fenders. The police personally delivered these beautiful bikes to the three brothers. The next day, Eugene Larry found the fourth bike on his front doorstep. It was the most ordinary, unadorned bicycle in the world. At least, that's the way it probably seemed to Eugene Larry in comparison with the three sets of wheels his next-door neighbors had." Senator Gaylord glanced at McManus. "Do you have any idea what happened next?"

"I'm afraid to imagine," McManus offered.

The Senator paraded around the room, strutting. "You know what he did," he said accusingly. "We all know what he did......the nigger stole. Not too far from where he lived, there was a Pep Boys. They were waiting for him. It happened on a Saturday. He arrived early, went directly to the bicycle department and without any ado, stuffed a shiny horn under his shirt. Needless to say, he was apprehended and arrested. I subsequently kept the case out of the reach of the juvenile authorities as I wasn't ready to lock him up yet. Nonetheless, I was overjoyed that my premise had worked so flawlessly and that, gentlemen, was the defining moment of my young life."

Everyone around the conference table was enthralled, visibly mesmerized by the menace, the awesome power of what they had just heard. It made cloning seem like hop-scotch. After the passing of the initial wave of fear and guilt, the men smiled at each other.

"I will desist from all the details, but my puppet is forty-eight years old and at my behest has spent a total of twenty-five of those years in prison at various times dating back to when he was fourteen." Senator Gaylord boasted. "I challenge any of you to top that." He grinned widely. "In the spirit of fairness, I must mention that it doesn't always have to be business with your puppet. While the main focus is to keep him in prison, I did devise some entertaining secondary games that I used as conditioning agents to keep my puppet tracked."

"Give us an example." It was McManus.

The Senator attempted modesty, but failed. The cockiness returned. "I made it impossible for him to have a relationship with a light-skinned black woman."

"How was that done?" Jack Torrence blurted.

"Put on your thinking caps, boys," Senator Gaylord laughed. "Remember the rats in a maze? They press a blue lever, they would be rewarded with a pellet of food. Press a red lever and they would be shocked. After so many times pressing the red lever and receiving a painful jolt, the rats became automatically conditioned to hate the color red. This is the wonderful technique I applied to Mr. Larry. Any time he approached or was approached by a light-skinned woman, well, let's say that something very unpleasant would occur."

"Like what?" Jack Torrence was very interested.

"His shock might be that he would get arrested afterwards or get his money stolen. Or even get chased by some vicious dogs let loose on him by a lil' ol' lady. Anything to associate bad luck to light-complexioned women. In short order, I had my puppet practically running for cover at the sight of such targeted women."

"Amazing," Jack Torrence gasped. "Simply amazing."

"I even forced him to drive only a certain model car. I did allow him to choose the color." The Senator laughed loudly.

"And we can do the same thing?" someone quizzed.

"All I can do," quipped Senator Gaylord, "is to offer you the power to do what I've done. Success is something you must determine."

"I'm in," Jack Torrence chimed. "Where do I sign up?"

"This is the deal. Each of you will head up a team that you will direct and train to head other teams." The Senator sipped from his cup of water. "Starting now, one out of every four black male babies born in the country must be earmarked for us for adoption as puppets. We will have well-qualified nurses and doctors in every major hospital in America. They will choose our puppets for us and quarterly a lottery will be held to apportion these babies out. You will be directly responsible for your puppets, but at no time are you to have any personal contact with them although they must be absolutely controlled and conditioned. I have no concerns about what side games you might devise to amuse yourselves, but this I am concerned with. Keep your puppets away from white women and have them prison-ready by their sixteenth birthday. Do each of you understand." He slapped the table hard. "Good!"

A round of drinks was poured.

"Using a base rate augmented with the annual expense of keeping and maintaining a prisoner while confined, I have deduced that you should receive a $10,000 bonus each time your puppet is locked up, provided the term of incarceration is greater than twelve months." The Senator smiled graciously. "Hell, he is your puppet. Feel free to run him in and out of prison as you see fit, however at sixty-five either let him stay locked up or leave him alone. From sixteen to sixty-five, that's quite a bit of a nest's egg if you play your cards right."

Another round of drinks was served.

"In the future, in an effort to corner the market on every available jailhouse dollar, we will get involved in supplying food, medicine, and cleaning supplies to the prisons throughout the nation. We'll establish independent trucking firms. I'll have dummy corporations set up in our behalf and the competition will be phased out. We'll have the whole shebang to ourselves."

"Here's to puppets", the men all said.

Halloween.

The participants had received their specially-delivered engraved invitations the day before. Both the envelopes and the stationery were fine, high-grade paper, and the engraved script was exquisite. Inside each envelope was a smaller envelope. **DO NOT OPEN** was stenciled in across the front. They were to be opened in Dallas at the conference. Not a single individual intended to be late. None were.

That evening after a round of drinks in the hotel bar, Senator Gaylord clamored aboard the elevator en route to the top floor meeting hall. At around the same time, from various rooms in the luxurious hotel, half a dozen men made the trek upstairs as well.

The entourage arrived. McManus, Torrence, Baldwin, Baxter and two others.

The Senator rocked back and forth on the balls of his feet. "After today, there will be no room to turn around. From this point on, gentlemen, I cannot tolerate any behavior that will, in any sense, undermine this venture." He cast a woeful glance at the men. "Your envelopes, please."

Staring at the envelopes, the men curiously, nervously looked at each other, then away, returning their eyes back to the envelopes. They briefly hovered over them as though they were souvenirs.

"Open them."

Compliance was instantaneous.

"The first puppets will be allotted this evening." The room burst with a bristling energy. "In the same way that each of you was carefully selected to spearhead this historic mission, so were your puppets. Their mission is no less important than yours so I assure you that extreme care went into the selection process." He paused. "For your information, all the puppets weighed in at birth at between seven to nine pounds. All puppets allotted you now and in the future will be healthy. If not, for any reason, you have my ironclad guarantee that I will replace the defective product and will provide you with a $50,000 indemnity. That's quite a rebate. To insure that we get at least fifty productive years from each puppet, we start a careful examination at birth. That is done so that you can reap healthy profits."

The men were informed that a special day care center had been recently established and that it was their duty to steer their puppets to it. Although there would be non-puppets in attendance, the care-takers of the facility would know who was who. The men were instructed to form a close working relationship with the day care facilitators.

"At no point," The Senator barked, "are you to relinquish control of your puppet to the facilitator. They work for you and if you are in any way lax or negligent in your duties, they will feel no remorse in reporting you. They get paid well and part of their job description is instant notification of any lapse on the part of any of you."

After enduring a brief, dramatic pause, the men were commanded to open the second envelope and to match their number with the number on the chalkboard. The Senator walked over, deliberately slow and tugged at the string. The exposed blank canvas covering rolled itself up, snapping shut at the top, revealing numbers. *And names.* The men craned their necks, searching for their numbers. Locating the numbers, they saw the names.

Puppets!

Warren Hill.....Lothario Cummings.....Vincent Taylor......William Sloan.....and others.

The men hurriedly associated names and numbers, individually scribbling the name of their puppet.

As the men left the conference room, the Senator provided them with a final piece of wisdom. "Just remember that they are only niggers," he said sagely. "The rest should be easy."

3

Jenners' Motion For Summary Judgment legally informed the Court that since no prima facie case could be made by the plaintiff that the claims should be dismissed. In his brief, he argued that the case should not proceed to trial simply because, as a matter of law, Safety Pins, had not, in any way, been negligent. He espoused that it was the mothers themselves who were negligent and to support this view, he had enlisted the testimony of two child-care experts.

The experts, both from Minnesota, had concluded that in black households headed by females, there existed an uncommonly high incidence of disrespect for authority prevalent among children, especially toddlers, raised in such households. The corresponding link was that these children were incapable of following instructions.

The report claimed that the highly pronounced strain of infantile non-conformity was a direct result of the mother's early neglect of the child. The second doctor verified these findings, adding that to find Safety Pins guilty would be like the USDA putting a Grade A sticker on defective meat and then getting mad at the supermarket for selling it. Hell, the product was defective when it left home!

Whether the brief had any merit or not didn't disturb Jenners. He just wanted to forewarn the lady lawyer that she was now in the deep end of the pool where the water was shark-infested.

Jenners begged the Court to schedule a date for oral arguments and then slipped the brief in the mail.

It arrived on Elizabeth's desk two days later. She studied it with fading optimism. She could appreciate a tough legal battle based on the merits of the case, but this was nothing more than a thinly-disguised mockery of not just the law, but African-Americans. She would accept the challenge. She filed for an extension of time and then made a phone call to a local Charlotte investigator.

The private investigator returned her call on Tuesday.

"Miss Sellers?"

"Yes."

"This is Smith."

"Yes, Lou, what did you get?"

"Nothing. There is no such company as that. It has never existed. Anywhere."

"And you're sure?"

"Definitely. If it had had a life span of only thirty minutes and had left a paper trail of any sort, I would have found it. My best guess is that Ronpis is or was a dummy organization. What it was set up for we'll never know since it is no longer around. If you come up with any more clues, feed them to me and I'll see what I can do. If I come up with anything more, you'll be the first to know, but quite frankly, Miss Sellers, I did a real thorough check this time."

"Thanks, Lou. Goodbye."

"Later."

Elizabeth rose from her desk and walked to the window. She loved the view, but this time her mind was elsewhere. She needed a hook, something that would give her the power to go toe-to-toe with the absurdness of Jenners' Summary Judgment Motion although she knew it was a bunch of crock, a meaningless jab. She rushed back to her desk. Made a call.

"Yes, Lou, this is Elizabeth Sellers again. Be a sweetheart and get me a profile on these four names. Also check out their mothers. What I'm looking for is a link between Ronpis and either the mothers or the sons. I'm trying to determine just how or why these four children were chosen to attend Safety Pins on a freebie. Get back with me as soon as you find out anything. The names are Vincent Taylor, Lothario Cummings, William Sloan, and Warren Hill."

On Friday.

"Miss Sellers?"

"Yes."

"This is what I've got. None of the mothers have any criminal priors. All have spotty employment records. All have had children before with the exception of Tamara Sloan. On the kids, all that appears on them is that they were all born at Presbyterian Hospital, and get this. They were all born on the same day, September 1st. After leaving Presby, all the boys went separate ways and nothing suggests that the mothers knew each other prior to this, even though it is possible they were aware of each other since Safety Pins was their collective day care provider."

"Nothing at all, I assume, about Ronpis?"

"Nothing."

"But when I spoke with the women, each of them told me specifically that they were approached by someone representing a company named Ronpis who gave each of them a day care voucher that would insure free enrollment of their children at Safety Pins until he was old enough to attend public school."

"I checked the enrollment record at Safety Pins and at various times, beginning with Warren Hill, all of them were registered. However under the section outlining payment of enrollment fees, private sponsor is listed." Lou Smith paused. "If the tuition was paid by some kind of stipend or company check, I could see who issued it and see what I could scare up from there."

"If it's paid by voucher....." Her voice trailed. "Thanks, Lou. Goodbye."

Initially, Elizabeth had been excited by her presumed defense against Jenners' scathing attack, but without Ronpis, she was on a 'fishing expedition'. Moreover, the deadline for her response approached swiftly. It had been her intention to use the good name and reputation of Ronpis to counter Jenners' approach that the children were nothing short of genetic morons. Damn. If only Ronpis existed. The mother of each child had said that their child had been chosen from a wide, diverse field of candidates by Ronpis which was a well-known company working under the auspices of The American Pediatrics Association. They all said that Ronpis sponsored only the best qualified babies.

Elizabeth recalled being told by Angie Cummings that the qualifying process was exacting. Data included, but was not limited to, all initial hospital records, follow-up check-ups, and the assessments of the handling physician. Once everything was complied, the data was packaged and shipped to Nevada. Here, the field of candidates was narrowed some more. Those who did not rate above the optimal standard were removed from any further consideration, but those surviving this grueling assessment had their portfolio sent to Washington. The final cut would be made there. Only those with overall superior marks in all categories were selected and awarded the free vouchers to attend Safety Pins, hailed by Ronpis as a 'very elite universe unto itself.'

After the very exhaustive study by a reputable agency such as Ronpis, there is no way Jenners could claim those boys were defective. Shit, Ronpis had all but certified them as super and had granted them the seal of approval from the loving hands of the APA. Once she would have alerted them to Jenners' claims, she would have it appear as an insult to them and then would have invited them to Court to protect their reputation. All she would have had to do was to unleash her dogs on Jenners and watch them chew his pet theory to pieces. But there was no Ronpis. Never had been one. Even the APA in whose name they had come had never heard of them.

In the back of her mind, Elizabeth strangely felt that she was stepping on the threshold of something big and dangerous, frightening. But she couldn't think about it. Her main concern was to prove that Safety Pins had been negligent and as a result was liable for the injuries sustained by her clients.

Despite this pledge to herself to remain focused, she was still enormously puzzled. Why would such an elaborate scam be set up just to lure four, young, black boys into this specific day care center? *Why?!* Was there something significant surrounding the fact that all the boys had been born on September 1st? If so, what?

"Something amazing is going on", Elizabeth muttered aloud.

Under no circumstances were these women, Deborah, Angie, Tamara, and Regina, ever supposed to have gotten together and find out they all had the same invisible sponsor, Ronpis, who was a sort of personal fairy godmother. Yet, the incompetence of Safety Pins had spoiled that.

Elizabeth made up her mind. After she finished with Jenners in Court, she would really find out what was going on. Once and for all.

It was a warm day for November, with blue skies and a shining sun, but Elizabeth had still worn a top coat. She felt cold. And tired. Sleep had been cruel too her and had stood her up like an errant date until the final seconds before dawn. Then she had gratefully dozed. Now, it was in this state of fatigue, offset by caffeine, that she was to face Judge Postman in response to Jenners' Summary Judgment Motion. Today, oral argument had been scheduled.

She entered the ancient building from the side entrance. She went slowly across the glistening waxed floor, her heels click-clacking as she walked through the cavernous lower level to the stairwell. She had never noticed an elevator.

The top floor was filled with empty, abandoned offices. She passed them all. The US Parole Office. Abandoned. The Internal Revenue Office. Empty. The US Courtroom. Waiting. She entered. 10:00 am. Time to get to work.

Elizabeth always thought of Lemon Pledge when she entered a courtroom. The interior of this one was all wood which was shined and burnished to a high gloss. She was forever careful not to touch anything. The Judge's perch, empty and elevated, rose at a right angle to the long, solid table where she would sit. She hefted her briefcase and laid it flat down, unsnapping the double claps. They made the familiar muted metallic pop. Twice.

Jenners arrived. Without thinking or knowing why, she glanced at her watch as if his being two minutes late would give her an edge. With him were two other men. They were either other attorneys or they were his experts. She would soon find out.

A menacing, hulking figure clad in black stepped into the courtroom through a side door. It was the Judge.

To mark the occasion, the bailiff bellowed. "All rise."

"Let's hear it," Judge Postman declared in a crisp and commanding tone. "And please, counsels, I warn you to stick to the issue at hand. Don't attempt to try the case this morning. We're not here for that." He stared over the rim of his glasses. "I'll tell you something else. I got a backlog of cases that has me snowed over for months. Either you guys settle up or go to trial as soon as possible. Upcoming cases will not be dragged along. I also will not tolerate any delaying tactics, or any untimely filed, irrelevant motions." He sat tall in his chair. "Are all witnesses present?"

"Yes," Jenners intoned.

"I have none."

The Judge, plus everyone else in the courtroom, stared at Elizabeth in surprise.

"Alright then." The Judge nodded at Jenners who stood stiffly. "Am I to understand, counselor, that it is your allegation that due to psychological reasons, your client, Safety Pins Day Care Center, is not liable for negligence even though children under their direct care suffered injury. Is that your interesting position?"

"I intend to prove just that, Your Honor, and after doing so will request that summary judgment be entered----"

"Call your first witness," Judge Postman butted in. "Save your speeches." He spoke to Elizabeth. "Since you saw fit to leave your witnesses at home, I take it that you intend to be so brilliant in your cross-examination that you will win in this fashion?"

"Yes, Your Honor. I intend to do just that."

"Mr. Jenners," Judge Postman said softly, "the Court will hear you now."

"Your Honor, for my first witness, I'd like to call----"

"Just call him, then, counselor. No need for dramatics. The gallery is empty."

"Yes, Your Honor." He walked to his table. "Dr. Harvens, would you please take the stand?" The young-looking, blond-haired man rose quietly. He was rather thin with long, angular arms and bony wrists that poked through the sleeves of his jacket.

"Please state your name for the Court?"

"Gunnar Harvens."

"And you are professionally?"

"A developmental psychobiologist from the University of Minnesota. I hold a doctorate in the field and I've been quite avid and active in my filed for over a decade."

"Would you say that during this time you have conducted extensive research in cognitive abuse in children and the adverse manner in which it affects these children as they progress in years?"

"I have indeed. In fact, it was I who presented and initiated the classic study into this field while I was a student in Germany."

"So rightly you are considered to be the leading expert on childhood disorders?"

Dr. Harvens feigned humility. "I concede that I am an expert."

"Would you explain then what happens in children with maladaptive responses?"

"Actually, it's what is known quite precisely as irregular cortisol levels. You see, excessive cortisol levels causes irreparable damage to the hippocampus."

"Let me interrupt for a second," Jenners pleaded. "If the hippocampus is somehow damaged, so what? There are known cases where individuals have been shot in the brain and still have gone on to live normal lives. Can it be than excessive cortisol is more devastating than a bullet in the brain?"

"Interesting hypothesis. At any rate, there are surgical procedures for the removal of bullets and any fragments, but it is not true with abuse. To date, and I doubt there will ever be a technique, surgical or otherwise, that can excise the damage done by abuse or neglect. In children where either or both are apparent, severe damage is precipitated in the brain's left hemisphere and it is here in this hemi that logical thought as well as language is processed."

"Hold on, now. Just wait a minute," Jenners insisted. "So if the language processing center is shut down, would that mean that children with left hemi disturbance would find it difficult to understand language, even their own tongue?"

Dr. Harvens became reflective. "There are a couple of things that come into play here. They may or may not understand, but even if they do understand, you have to take into account that there is no corresponding logical thought by which to filter the information into the appropriate channels of right or wrong."

"So if you told a child to remain seated or you'll get eaten by a polar bear, what kind of effect would that have on the child?"

"Again, it's an all or nothing proposition. Such a warning could have no effect whatever on the child or it could mean everything. Since the left hemisphere in kids of abuse have fewer nerve cell connections, they are most likely to be self-destructive with the result that they may want to get eaten by a polar bear."

"So their disobedience is a direct result of a self-destructive tendency induced by parental abuse and neglect?"

"Precisely."

Jenners walked to the table. He had a seat. "Please explain the mechanics of irregular cortisol levels and its effect on children."

"Most people of the world are aware of Post-Traumatic Stress Disorder from the records and reports of soldiers returning to civilian life after observing combat duty. Now, it is generally recognized that PTSD is just as pronounced in children who are traumatized from abuse and neglect, especially where violence is present. It does not have to be repeated episodes of violence; a single traumatic experience can be enough to alter the brain's chemistry with dire consequences later in life. These kids conversely become victims of high blood pressure, high resting heart rates, etc.. In a sense, they over-react to everything. Everything, in turns, threatens them and in this state of hyperawareness, the kids can't absorb information concretely. So much time is invested in the constant being-on-guard for threats that their brain fails to develop language and problem-solving skills."

"So," Jenners concluded, "abnormal kids apt to act as such even in a normal environment such as a day care facility?"

"That is correct. The emotional damage is set at home. That is where the negligence originated. The ultimate culprit is the home, the parents are mainly responsible."

By the time Jenners had finished with his direct examination, Elizabeth was fighting to restrain her anger. She was totally incensed by the absurdity of the allegations, even more so at the cool, detached manner in which Dr. Harvens had delivered his careful, laid-back testimony.

It was too late now, but she wished she had spent money to hire an expert of her own. Too late for regrets now. She had to act as her own authority and given the countless hours she had spent quietly establishing a counterpoint, she felt vaguely qualified to dissect both doctors and their bogus research. Even though she had slept little the night before, surges of adrenaline began to race through her body, offering rejuvenation. She found her resolve revitalized. She rose. She approached the witness stand. She spoke.

"To begin with, Dr. Harvens, I have one very important question for you. In what environment is Post-Traumatic Stress Disorder most likely to be induced?"

"Most frequently in war-torn countries where violence is a daily occurrence."

"So you conclude that America is war-torn?"

"No, I never said that."

"I object," Jenners shouted. "That calls for an irrelevant observation."

Elizabeth looked at the Judge.

"Proceed." Judge Postman glared at Jenners.

"Well, do you reckon the black neighborhoods of Charlotte to be torn by war and civil strife?"

"Dr. Harvens appeared sheepish. "I cannot realistically answer that question with specific regard to this city because---"

"You have never been in a black Charlotte neighborhood. Is that correct?"

"Yes, that is correct. But certain ghettoes and slums in this country possess identical characteristics of a war zone."

"While I do not dispute that, I need to have specifics about Charlotte. In your field of endeavor, Dr. Harvens, you have the luxury to generalize. In law, we are afforded no such grant. We deal with specifics. This case specifically deals with Safety Pins Day Care Center in Charlotte. The victims are specifically from Charlotte, so in line with those specs I'd like to see your charts and graphs that specifically delineates the incidence of PTSD in children from black neighborhoods in Charlotte."

"I object." It was Jenners.

"Overruled." It was the Judge.

"I cannot point to the rate of incidence among any particular neighborhoods, let alone this city."

"So it may be that the symptoms you universally describe do not or may not exist among black children in Charlotte?"

"If there is abuse, then I'm sure it exists."

Elizabeth sighed. "I'm eager to point out to the Court that among my clients, there is no record at all of abuse. No tell-tale signs of neglect." She went to her briefcase and removed some papers which she distributed. "This," she remarked,"is a breakdown of the neighborhoods where my clients live. You will notice the demographics include average economic factors which are standard. Domestic violence is no more rife in these neighborhoods than elsewhere in the city and totally absent from the homes of my clients. Over the last three years, there have only been two murders combined for all the neighborhoods, no major drug busts have occurred there and the only shootouts are on television. This hardly fits your image of a war zone."

"Absent research----"

"The answer is no, isn't it?'

"The answer is no." Dr. Harvens' voice was flat.

The denial encouraged Elizabeth. In fact she felt confident she had made her point. She decided not to press on. "I have no further questions," she said.

Once dismissed from the witness box, Dr. Harvens rushed to take his seat beside Jenners. He cast a weary glance at Dr. Ostig, the other expert.

"Counselor Jenners," Judge Postman intoned solemnly. "Is the testimony of your second witness radically different from that of Dr. Harvens or does he simply intend to support and bolster what has already been said? If he has nothing short of revolutionary to expound upon, then let's not waste time."

Jenners stood erect, facing the Judge, nodding graciously to Elizabeth. "Your Honor," he stated blandly, "I have nothing further for the Court at this time."

"Your Motion," the Judge imparted with equal solemnity, "is hereby dismissed." He looked over the top of his spectacles. "Be ready for trial in six months. Both of you." He banged his gavel. "Court is adjourned."

On the first Sunday after Veteran's Day, Regina Taylor went to visit her babies' daddy. Piedmont Correctional Center was a high-rise prison about forty-five miles from Charlotte, located in Rowan County. From the parking lot, it looked deceptively like a hospital. Tony, her boyfriend, called it a pretty coffin, a tomb for the living dead.

Usually, when she was permitted through all the checkpoints and was allowed to enter the visitation room, there was a long wait for Tony. He had to get "pretty" for her. As it turned out, this time, he was there in a flash. Strikingly handsome.

"Hiya, babe," he exclaimed joyfully, hugging her. "Damn, you look good."

Their lips met, touched, thereby using up one of their two sanctioned kisses. They'd have one for the road.

"How's my boys?"

"They are both okay," Regina responded. "Why didn't you want me to bring them? You know you enjoy seeing them."

"I didn't want no distraction, babe. Just me and you. Gotta talk some stuff over and if things go right, if you really in my corner, then none of you will ever have to come visit me in this place no mo'." He squeezed her hands tightly. "I got a shot to be free, babe, but you gotta help me."

Regina lowered her head, whispering softly. "Tony, you know I love you, but I pray you not gonna ask me to help you escape." Her voice was sad. "Please, Tony, don't do that too me." She squeezed his hand back, seeking reassurance. "Tony."

"Naw, babe, it ain't nuthin' like that.

Regina relaxed.

"And it's simple and inexpensive."

Regina brightened. This was sounding better all the time. If getting her man free was that simple, then she felt compelled to do her part. She had been without a man for three years.

"You don't want me to stay in here, do you?" Tony inquired.

"Don't ask me no silly questions like that, boy. You know, I want you home with me and our sons. What do I have to do? Is it completely legal?"

"Yeah, girl, I done tole you that. I wouldn't ask you to do nuthin' wrong. Already ain't no daddy in the house. You think I want the Mama gone too? Girl, think."

"Okay, okay. What you want me to do?"

Tony took a deep breath. "You know that if you turn me down that I'll be stuck in here for another five years. Already done been gone three. You know that, right?"

"Just tell me, Tony. Please."

"Okay, here it is. Do you remember when I called you Wednesday?"

"Umm hmm."

"Well, my case worker let me call. He the one that sent for me, had me come to his office. We bullshitted for a second or two, talking 'bout them bum-ass Panthers. Then he tells me that some people in DC wanting to look out for me. Said they wanted to get me out."

Regina was getting excited. She smiled.

"Mr. Preston, my case worker, told me that these people would help me once I got out, that they would make it easy for us to get on Section 8 and get us a brick crib with a fireplace, a den, and a big backyard. And that ain't all. Mr. Preston said they would even hook me up with a small business loan so we could start our own business."

Regina was bursting with joy. She beamed brightly.

"Don't that sound good," Tony prodded. "And all this can be all ours---right away---*if you drop your lawsuit against that day care center!*"

Regina's hopes were dashed. She frowned.

"Our son almost died because of those people and you want me to forget about it? You want me to act like nothing happened."

"I'm not asking you to forget, babe, because the pain of what happened will always be there, but what will going to court prove? If it's money you after, we'll have our own business. Ain't that good enough? Going to Court fighting these white folk won't bring me home."

"I can't believe you just want me to give up and forget that these people almost caused our son his life."

"It didn't happen, though. Vincent didn't die. He is as alive as we are. I admit it, babe, those day care people were negligent, but what about you? If you leave me in here when you can get me out, you know what I call that? Negligence. That same shit the crackers did with Vincent, neglecting him, is the same shit you'd be doing to me, except I won't have no damn body to find me in the nick of time. Won't be no lifesaver for me. I'll be dead, babe. Deader than a motherfucka."

Regina stared coldly. "I love you, but I need stormy weather money for me and my sons. What insurance can you give me that you won't go south on me again like you did the last time you got out? How do I know I can depend on you this time? How can I be sure of what you gonna do?"

"How can you be sure you gonna win in Court? You might not get shit."

Regina stood to leave.

"So it's like that huh, bitch?"

Regina stormed out of the visiting room.

In mid-November, Elizabeth received an urgent phone call from Regina Taylor whom she scheduled in for a 2:30pm appointment.

As always, Regina was prompt. Elizabeth smiled. They hugged warmly and without delay Elizabeth detected a stiffness, never apparent before. This vague undercurrent alerted Elizabeth to a change in Regina, a subtle hint that was dark and negative. It clung to the woman even more indelibly than the expensive perfume she wore. Even that was new, Elizabeth noted.

Elizabeth stepped back and before seating herself closely regarded Regina. New clothes. Freshly-coiffed hair. Expensive perfume.

"What did you do," Elizabeth joked, "make Christmas come before Thanksgiving?"

Regina only smiled. She was nervous and sought relief by picking her finely-sculpted fingernails. She took a long breath.

"Well," Elizabeth continued, "what can I do for you?"

Regina stared first at Elizabeth, then at the candy dish. She slowly chose a brightly-wrapped piece of toffee and ritually unwrapped it as though it was ambrosia, extending the process beyond any meaningful craving for candy. At last, she placed the mound of candy on her tongue, twisting the wrapper between her dainty fingers. "Have you read the newspaper?"

Elizabeth admitted that she hadn't.

"Listened to the news?"

Again, the answer was no.

"Has anyone told you?"

"No, Regina, I haven' read the paper, heard the news, and no one has told me anything. So I guess the job is yours." Elizabeth smiled. "Whatever has happened, I imagine everyone concerned felt that no one was better qualified to tell the news than you----and here you are." Elizabeth clasped her hands together. "You see how things work sometimes."

"Angie is dead," Regina blurted.

"*What!?*" Elizabeth's eyes stretched wide in disbelief.

"Angie is dead. Lothario too."

"*How? What happened? When?*"

"They were on a plane," Regina sobbed. "The plane crashed." She dabbed at her eyes. "It's all in the papers, all in the news."

Elizabeth quickly crossed the office to a dumbwaiter, filled two cups and came back to her desk, reaching Regina some water. "When did this happen?"

"Late last night. They released some of the names of the people who had died. It was like Angie's and

Lothario's names jumped out at me. I started screaming. I just lost control until Tony---".

"*Tony*?!" Elizabeth interrupted. "Tony's home?"

Regina glanced at her paper cup. "That's something else I guess we gotta talk about."

When Regina finished, Elizabeth was no longer in a bright mood. It would do no good to suggest that Regina had shown poor judgment in her decision or that she should have conferred with her before making such a blunder. To do so would have insisted that Tony wasn't worth saving. As for Angie and Lothario, that was a done deal also.

"So," Elizabeth asked, "Tony doesn't know who these people in Washington are?"

"No. Everything was handled by his case-worker."

"What's that case worker's name?"

Regina's eyes grew mildly suspicious. "You not gonna make trouble, are you? I know you got a man. I felt I was deserving of one to. Is that a crime, wanting somebody to come home to?"

"No, sista, wanting to be loved is no crime and I don't intend to cause you or Tony any problems, but I'm still obligated to this case and now I see that something much bigger is going on than just negligence."

"Well, I wish you luck. I'm sorry that I couldn't see this through to the end."

Elizabeth shrugged. "Trust me. I understand. Who can resist when Santa Claus comes early."

Long after Regina had gone, Elizabeth made no mention to herself about how the sudden and untimely withdrawal of two of her clients would affect her trial strategy. She still had enough time to improvise. What really occupied her thoughts was who was the force behind Safety Pins. What were they out to do?

The next few weeks would be critical in getting her case shaped up and pared down to trail size so she could spoon-feed the jurors. Losing clients robbed the case of some of its emotional power and adversely thinned the line she intended to thread to demonstrate a telling pattern of neglect and incompetence. Now, thanks to Santa and Satan, she had been resourcefully deprived of the opportunity to play upon the sympathy of the jurors.

Packing it in for the evening, Elizabeth felt she could still win the case stripped down to its bare bones essence. Since she could no longer depend on the emotional punch of the evidence, she would have to drum up additional evidence and testimony to prove that this was much more than two little boys walking out into traffic and getting hit.

She also knew that if she was going to do that, then she would have to be able to rip the mask off of the monster behind Safety Pins.

5

Senator Gaylord rose stiffly after he was introduced and strode boldly to the stage. The small auditorium was packed.

"We have so many business opportunities at this moment," he began, "that if crime went on a vacation for a while, it wouldn't hurt us. Presently, we have more than enough convicts to spread around to keep our bottom line healthy, but we must consider the future."

Everyone knew what was coming next. Statistics. And they were right.

"The arrest record among 10-17 year old black males has jumped 80%. The good news about this is that forty states now allow juveniles as young as thirteen to be tried as adults." Gaylord challenged the lobbyists. "Bring me five more states and you will have your just rewards. That I promise you. Help me pass this youth crime punishment bill and I will put cash in your pockets." He turned his attention back to the general audience. "Considering the rate teenage niggers are killing each other, we need to start profiting off them at thirteen rather than sixteen. Those extra years will help defray any untimely losses due to homicide." Gaylord grinned. "I would rather have then locked up than buried."

The Senator spoke on the fact that more money was spent on prison construction than on education. Starting in 1987, state government spending for prison increased 60% while during that same period, spending on higher education decreased.

"Honest Abe Lincoln freed the slaves," Gaylord preached, "and now it's our job to round them up again." He chuckled. "Only this time the prison will be the plantation and the warden will be the Massa." Gaylord laughed loudly. He stopped abruptly. "I offer a humble apology for our little debacle at Safety Pins. It will soon be set straight." He glanced at Jenners who simply nodded his head slightly at first, but when he noticed the Senator still watching him, wagged it more vigorously. Satisfied, Gaylord moved on. "Once lazy, black mothers are coaxed off the welfare rolls and pushed, kicking and screaming, if need be, into the job market, state legislators will be motivated to provide day care to this new crop of workers. That's where Safety Pins will come in. You see, Safety Pins is merely the first step in the long chain of institutionalization required to get your puppets ready for the real market---the chain-gang. With this brand of quality control, the sky is the limit."

The Senator moved to the side of the podium and called a doctor to the stage. The doctor hurriedly rushed up. He stood only a few feet away from the Senator, directing everyone's attention to the chalkboard. His eyes lingered carefully on the impassive face of the Senator and then darted back to the board.

"Our colleague and friend, the Honorable Senator Gaylord," the doctor began in a voice that sounded like cracked glass on concrete, "is interested in healthy, robust specimens, puppets, I think you call them. In any event, I assure each of you that there will be no difficulty in this arena." He pointed to a chart. "We have prenatal tests for 450 genetic diseases. These tests allow us to know well in advance if a fetus is healthy or not. These tests are routine which makes our choices rather simple as we can avoid the babies carrying mutated genes."

All of this was very depressing to James Baxter whose own son, Jamie, had been born with spinal bifuda, an opening in the spinal cord. At the time, genetic testing was not so prevalent and his wife had turned down aminocentestis tests because of the risks of miscarriage. Now, his only son would grow up being ostracized. He would face blatant discrimination from insurers and employers just like....he recoiled at the thought. His son would be discriminated in much the same way as niggers were. He had never made that connection before. Suddenly, deep down, he had a pang of conscience. Could it be that he was on the wrong side of the fence?

The doctor continued. "There are presently three major categories of genetic testing and by using them, it is possible to detect a large number of birth defects easily, so selecting healthy specimens should be no problem. No problem at all."

"So there you have it, gentlemen," Gaylord roared, "my ironclad guarantee of healthy puppets." He fixed his gaze on Felix Baldwin. "You'll have to sit the next exercise out since you are out of a puppet, but since his death was beyond your absolute control, you'll receive a $10,000 bonus to compensate your untimely loss." Gaylord grinned slyly. "Some people shouldn't get on planes."

McManus, Torrence, Baxter, some of the others glared at Baldwin. They were envious. Who knew that ten thousand dollars could be made so easily?

"Now that we have totally eliminated any prenatal hazards to your puppets," Gaylord went on to say, "they should make it home in tip-top condition, miniature Cam Newtons and Kobe Bryants, but this is where you will have to step in to make sure the environment is tightly controlled. Our specifications are plenty of dope, illiteracy, median or below average poverty, and lot of nappy-headed niggers born out of wedlock." He waved his hands absently. "You get the picture, I'm sure. And now for some homework." He stared into the audience.

"Who has Warren Hill as a puppet?" A hand shot up. Torrence. The Senator nodded in his direction. "I want the mother to lose her job. What about Vincent Taylor? Who has him?" Another hand shot up. Gaylord thought briefly. He winced. "I want that nigger daddy of his, Tony, back in jail." He glanced at his watch. "That's all, folks."

When Elizabeth arrived at the office on Monday, she could tell by the skeptical manner by which the strange man glanced at her that he was there to see her. Despite the fact that he was smiling as he continued to chat with George Bailey, another partner in the firm, she developed, almost immediately, a private sense of foreboding.

She made it to her office without the muffled sounds of approaching footsteps behind her, but this did not soften her premonitions. She knew the man was someone's hired gun---or lackey. She punched up the secretary and chatted, thinking she could perhaps learn something through her, but the secretary knew nothing except that he had just popped up out of nowhere. He had no appointment.

In the midst of her preoccupation, the expected knock on her door came. Through the glass panels on either sides of her office door, she saw the thin, angular form of Bailey gesturing at her as if to say "company's present". She opened the door and was surprised to see Jenners. Along with Bailey and the strange man, he entered the office. All four stood until after introductions and the customary shaking of hands, the proverbial pre-emptive first strike to establish dominance. Elizabeth pressed hard, her grip unladylike and firm. The strange man, Foster Bourne, caught off-guard by the power, smiled demurely, acknowledging that he had been bested in this initial test of wills.

Bailey saw the men seated and departed. He left the door slightly ajar, not quite closing it, a sure sign to Elizabeth that he subtly recommended caution. She didn't, however, require any hints. She would approach this session with the tenacity of a pit-bull whose domain had been invaded. If things went downhill, she wouldn't feel sorry for any damages done. After all, they had brought the fight to her.

Jenners effected the posture of a cherry-natured by-stander. He selfishly recognized no need to draw fire upon himself unnecessarily. That would be his due during the trial. He made it clear that this was not his fight and to put emphasis on his neutrality begged to use the restroom.

It turned out that Bourne was a congressional aide. He simply desired, as he put it, to demonstrate that she was meddling in affairs of state that didn't concern her either personally of professionally. Hearing that, Jenners immediately fled from the room, covering his ears. He knew what was coming. Fireworks!

"In Washington," Bourne continued, "we have a recurring problem with locals wanting to dial up a congressional hearing or investigation every time someone sneezes and doesn't cover their mouth. A lot of money gets wasted like that. Furthermore," he scolded, "what gave you the right to conduct your own personal inquisition against Mr. Preston at the Piedmont Correctional Center? The man was doing nothing more than following instructions."

"Whose instructions?" Elizabeth demanded. "That was my whole point and I'd still like to know why Washington was so interested in a local convict named Tony Albert." She stared Bourne in his eyes. "Or maybe no one was interested in Mr. Albert's welfare. Maybe Washington was very much concerned about the welfare of Safety Pins Day Care Center. Concerned enough to cut a deal to get Tony Albert released provided he could get the mother of their son, who was injured at Safety Pins, to drop her lawsuit."

Bourne shook his head in disbelief. "Oh, no," he groaned, "not another conspiracy theory." He leaned back in his chair, crossing his legs at the ankles. Elizabeth sized him up. Early thirties. A tall, chubby fall guy was her conclusion. "What's with this national obsession," he continued, "for the invention of a conspiracy whenever something is not to one's liking."

Elizabeth still stared. "It appears that the American public is smarter than you think. Anyway, Mr. Bourne, who sent you? That, quite possibly, is the man or woman I need to speak with."

"It you really must know, Miss Sellers, I personally arranged for the release of Mr. Albert from prison."

"Why?"

"It's not what you suspect. Actually, I'm on a panel consisting of individuals from the Social Security Administration and we have the responsibility of enacting the regulations of The Children's Disability Program." He winced. "We're not villains, but close to 100,00 disabled children will become ineligible to receive payments due to new stipulations. Many on the panel, myself included, realized that many children from low-income homes would be treated unfairly so we decided to conduct a case by case review."

Elizabeth was attentive, listening. She tried to disguise her interest with a put-on air of mistrust. Of course, she had no actual knowledge of these cuts, but did recall hearing about them on WCNC as she watched the 11:00 news.

"It was during this review, Miss Sellers, that we came across the file of Vincent Taylor whose case was submitted initially by the mental health division of Social Services right here in Charlotte. We instantly knew that the child didn't qualify and since he was not a prior recipient, there was not much we could do technically, but we were not without our resources." Bourne played with his hands, intertwining them, forming a bridge. "Do you know what we did, Miss Sellers?"

Silence.

"His diagnosis was termed minimal in regards to the level of brain damage and subsequent mental disability so, Miss Sellers, we opted for something a wee bit more unconventional. We knew that it would not be easy to care for Master Taylor if, by chance, his condition deteriorated, and when we discovered that the only income came from his mother, we, with myself in the lead, set the machinery in motion to get the father out of prison so he could support his family. The release was not compensation or payment for anything. It was done to help provide the supplemental income that the government was compelled to deny his son. Via Vocational Rehabilitation, Mr. Albert was granted a loan to start his own business. This is guaranteed income." Bourne sat tall. "Tony Albert was merely the first person to be released in such a fashion, but there will be more. These children need all the assistance they can get. Do you not agree, Miss Sellers?"

"Have you ever heard of Ronpis?"

"No. I represent the interests of disabled children and I'm sorry if I said or did nothing to enhance your budding conspiracy notion." He sighed impatiently. "Are there any more questions, Miss Sellers?"

Elizabeth rose rigidly. "Thank you for coming.

Jury selection had nothing to do with technical virtuosity or theatrical flair. It was purely intuitive, the phase of a trial where everything began long before the first shred of evidence was even presented. This was absolute Zen where the opposing counsels tried to plumb the depths of the human psyche, searching for kindred spirits, hoping to stack the deck in their psychological favor.

In essence, the jurors were the face of the trial, especially in a civil case. No matter how much the media or the public hated or loved any particular witness or despite how charming or culpable that witness may prove to be, in the end, it would be the jury, that faceless face that peered our from behind their impassive masks of assumed impartiality, who would decide. In a trial, once the preliminaries had been settled, everything else would be dedicated to them. The preening, the preaching, and the pomp were all geared to turn them against the other guy's lawyer, and by extension, the other guy.

From countless lawyers before her, Elizabeth had inherited the knowledge that even the strongest case could be weakened by a tainted jury. Unless you were extremely careful in your jury selection, you could bury yourself because once you permitted them to be impaneled, you relinquished all control over them. There were no guarantees. The Judge was commanded to be impartial. Lawyers were bound by ethics, and the witnesses were tied to a sworn oath. The jury. Well, they could believe whatever they wanted to. Evidence, be damned.

After Jenners' Motion for a change of venue had been denied, Judge Postman addressed the jury pool collectively. He commenced his paternal lecture with an admonition of what civic duty and pride dictated, how esteemed it was to be a decider of truth.

During the lecture, Elizabeth never glanced at Jenners. For the time being, he was nothing more than an expensive charcoal grey suit. Her focus was glued to the potential jurors, busily deciphering facial expressions, shifting eye movements, nervous tics; anything to allow her a glimpse of that person's inner being. As the Judge outlined the vivid details of the case to be, Elizabeth brazenly gawked at the jury box, lashing out with invisible feelers, searching for sympathy. She fragmented, dissected, and compartmentalized each of the men and women mentally until she had no doubts as to which of these citizens she would prey upon to be the personal torch-bearers of her legal angst.

"Do any of you wish to be excused for whatever reason?" the Judge wanted to know.

Three men. One women. Go, they were told.

"After listening to my description of the case, do any of you feel it will be too complicated for you to understand?"

A beefy, white man raised his hand. He was acknowledged. "My problem is the reverse, Your Honor. The case is so simple, that's it clear who the guilty party is."

"And you have already decided the case based on what you have already heard?"

"That is correct, Your Honor."

"You are excused," the Judge ordered.

Day one ended.

The following day, three more people were impaneled. Six jurors. Now, the hunt on was for six alternates. By noon, Elizabeth was left holding a single preemptory challenge. She would use it wisely. Jenners had gambled all his away, a riverboat gambler, hoping to steal the ace from off the bottom of the deck. He studied her critically.

The complexion of the jury was being colored in, a slow connect-a-dot of man, woman, black, white. The ebb and flow, the nuances of each choice slowly fleshing itself out. From out of this varied mix, both lawyers would attempt to fashion a melting pot, a cauldron from which they would draw sympathy. Or blood.

By the end of the day, four more candidates had been dismissed and with almost no time left before adjourning court for the evening, all was well. The twelve were impaneled. Elizabeth looked at the main jurors, studying them. She did the same for the alternates. She moaned a little bit inside. She liked the second string better. Too late now. There was no conceivable way for her to bench the starting jurors and to send in the scrubs. Damn!

Trial would begin next week.

Trial Day!

For Elizabeth, the chirping and the warbling of the birds trumpeted through the morning like a clarion call, her call to arms. She kicked the covers off her, rolled over, growled. Today was not the day to be timid or indecisive. She growled again. The tigress in her was ready, alert, claws unsheathed.

She prowled the morning, opening up the day, filling up all the cracks of time. The brisk cold shower cleared her head and helped dissolve any and all previously undisclosed cells of nervousness. She wanted nothing to compete with the positive power she felt coursing through her body. Once more, she growled.

She mentally rehearsed her uncomplicated trial strategy, paying particular interest to its shortcomings, counseling herself that nonetheless she would energetically gain the clear advantage. She almost growled again. Instead, she did two things at once. Dressed. Drank coffee.

By the time she entered the Courtroom, it was alive with people. There were no empties. Before she could reach the plaintiff's table, her clients arrived and moments later, so did the opposition, Hilton Jenners III.

Even though he had not yet emerged, everyone knew where the Judge was. Everyone was accounted for. The press and the media had gobbled up all the front row in-your-face-seats. Behind this privileged class of professional gawkers sat the Others. That's how it was at a good event, whether a boxing match or a trial. The VIPs. The Others.

The Courtroom buzzed, a full-tilt boogie of whispers and muffled coughing. Then at 10:15 in walked the Judge.

"All rise."

Being officially seated, one more muffled drone of anticipation flooded across the courtroom and then ceased to be.

Elizabeth would draw first blood. She presented her opening statement. "Would you indulge me for a little while," she began, speaking to the jury. "Indulge me as I humbly request that you go on a brief mental journey back... back" she muttered softly, "back into time. Imagine yourself a little child again, can you do that? Make yourself young again." She smiled, closing her eyes. "See how easy that was?" She paced back and forth across the courtroom. "When you're three years old, you depend on Mommy and Daddy to provide for you, to take care of you, and since they love you, this is exactly what they do. They take extra good care of you. But because of bills, Mommy and Daddy will have to go to work. Now, in the good old days, your parents wouldn't leave their precious cargo---you---with just anyone. Not hardly. What your parents would do on their way to work would be to drop you off at grandmother's house." She paused. "Grandmother." She let the word sink in. "More unconditional love for you there. While Mommy and Daddy worked, they knew you were in excellent hands. Why? Grandmother had you. They could reflect back on all the love they had gotten from this wonderful woman and knew there was more than enough left for you. Oh, what a relief it was to know that in their absence, their young one was getting loved. They knew that it felt extremely good to you as well." Elizabeth smiled. "Good love is like that." She stopped pacing. "But along the way to progress, something happened. Things changed. Day Care Centers started popping up, vying for our young, begging to take the place of grandmother, but who can substitute for granny? Such audacity," Elizabeth proclaimed. "Grandmother is personal. Day Care is a business. As with all things corporate, the concern is with their bottom line, not if your bottom is dry or not. Love gets lost in the lust for money. They want more heads in the romper room. After all, you're just a stranger passing through on their way to a paycheck.

That's what they're familiar with; money. Not your face. Not your individual needs. Not your safety."

For the better part of thirty minutes, Elizabeth preached, taught, scolded, and castigated. She painted word pictures, vivid and alive. She heaped scorn upon an industry that dared take the place of wonderful, loving grandmothers, and when she served up the boys, showing their scars and wounds, explaining how the jurors could heal them, women dabbed at their eyes while men dropped their heads.

When Elizabeth sat down, Jenners was ashen white.

The Judge ordered a break. He banged his gavel.

That decided it. That powerful opening statement left no doubt in Jenners' mind that he had to drag this out, to put as much distance between the verdict and that damned speech as possible, hoping that by then the jury would have forgotten it.

Was that possible?

When he rose to deliver his opening statement, everyone in the courtroom craned their necks, watching him intently. This had better be good, Jenners knew. When he first heard his voice, he wished he could have snatched the sound back. It was too high-pitched. He coughed, deepening his tone. "This is America and from the time of Virginia Dare, the first child of this country, America has fought hard to care for its young. Laws were enacted to give children guaranteed rights. It was decided quite some time ago that when it came to the welfare of the children that nothing would be left to chance. It was this same concern that established prenatal care, that established pediatric hospitals, and that put reforms in place such as Aid for Dependent Children. All of this simply for the love of children and that's why we have day care." Jenners stood in front of the jury box. "Day care didn't arise to challenge the warmth and affection of grandmothers. No. Instead, day care is the personification of grandmother evolved. In the same way that the wheel evolved into the horse and buggy into the car, day care centers are the evolution of grandmother's house." He started pacing. "Kids," he grinned, "will be kids and not even the most vigilant granny could save us from our countless scrapes and bruises. They sometimes just happened. No one blamed grandmother because everyone knew that cuts and bruises were as much a part of a baby's evolution as baby teeth and bronzed shoes."

There wasn't much further he could go with this line of argument. Even if he could move the jury to the premise of viewing Safety Pins as a capitalistic extension of Granma's hands, Jenners clearly understood the inherent futility of begging educated adults to accept scrapes and bruises and then infer that getting run over by a speeding car was just as innocent. Jenners refused to hang himself.

The bitch had won the opening round.

Commodore Thatcher had been on the stand for almost an hour. He was an administrative inspector for the Mecklenburg County Licensing Authority who had provided Safety Pins with accreditation. He and Jenners were establishing the finer points of accreditation and providing valid proof that Safety Pins was indeed operating under approved license.

Thatcher sat back in the chair, his jacket open, showing off a tan tie overlaying a brown shirt. His hair was parted down the middle with mousse and then combed over his ears. He was a medium-built man. Brown eyes. Effeminate voice. Smart.

"Did you personally send someone out to inspect the Safety Pins facility?"

"Oh, no," Thatcher declared. "I took responsibility for the inspection and performed it personally. The investigation was thorough and complete, I assure you."

Jenners rushed to a cart containing various exhibits that he had every intention of introducing into evidence. Grabbing a partially crinkled sheet of paper enclosed in a plastic folder, he strode towards the witness.

"Will you please identify this for the court?"

"This," Thatcher acknowledged, reaching for the paper, "is my checklist."

"What purpose, if any, does it serve?'"

"As I inspect the premises of a facility which had legally applied---"

Jenners stopped him. "You mean that before you even step foot onto a premise to conduct an inspection, you must have received, in your hands, a legal application?"

"Yes, and I'm quite sure that if you dig a little deeper in that cart, you should find the Safety Pins application."

Jenners located the document and turned sheepishly to the jury, waving the application at them. His voice sounded pained. "Isn't it wonderful the way the licensing board does things? No matter who you are. No matter how noble your mission, you must, by law, file an application for inspection which is all kept on file." He turned to the witness. "So even before Safety Pins filed for this application, they had to feel they could pass muster?"

"Objection, Your Honor," Elizabeth intoned. "That requires Mr. Thatcher to be able to deduce what another is thinking."

"Not quite, Your Honor," Jenners blurted before the Judge could rule. "I merely ask for his personal opinion as to what a particular piece of paper implied. Not that he read someone's mind."

"Overruled. Answer the question, Mr. Thatcher."

"Yes, the application usually carries the presumption of readiness. It's like going to take the road test for your driver's license. No one twists your arm to apply, so you go when you're ready. You do it knowing you can pass. Why go otherwise?"

"Then what?"

"I set the inspection date."

The application, once admitted into evidence, freely circulated throughout the jury box. The checklist used by Thatcher also made the rounds among the jurors. Thatcher testified that each item or box checked indicated that the area had been deemed satisfactory. The checklist covered such areas as entrances, exits, emergency doors, pest control, lights, menu supervision and a host of other minor and major areas of concerns.

Next came the accreditation license. It too was signed by Commodore Thatcher with an impeccable flourish of loops and over-sized letters. These documents were only the technical underpinnings of the case. Jenners simply wanted to establish that Safety Pins was on-the-level legal. That didn't bother Elizabeth. This evidence was crucial to Jenners' case. Not hers.

Elizabeth rose to face the witness.

"Mr. Thatcher, during your tours, what sort of safety concerns are you inclined to pay attention too?"

"All of them."

"But isn't safety maintenance more than just paying attention to physical barriers. What about the mental barriers to safety that is posed by the incompetence of the employees who administer to the children." Elizabeth smiled. "Even with the best sprinkler system available, it wouldn't be of any benefit to the safety of the children if the day care provider didn't know how to activate it."

Thatcher snickered. "Today, most sprinkler systems work automatically."

Elizabeth matched his snicker. "Still, if the employee didn't have the knowledge of how to properly formulate or follow an escape plan in case of an emergency, would this not pose a safety consideration?"

Thatcher sputtered. "I-I don't inspect employees. I inspect the physical plant."

"So even if you certify the building as safe, there still could exist real safety hazards due to human incompetence?"

"Again, my assurance is that----."

Elizabeth pressed the attack. "You certify that an empty building is safe. What about when that building is filled with guileless children and an inept facilitator?"

Thatcher's hand flew to his face.

"Isn't it true, Mr. Thatcher that your inspection guarantees the safety of the building, not the safety of the children who will occupy the building? In essence, your accreditation speaks highly of concrete and stone, the building, but it is silent when it comes to the flesh and bones of children?"

Thatcher just sat there, stone-faced. Almost like a building.

Julia Robertson looked healthy, robust, full of the outdoors and fresh air. She seemed more suited to be a mountain tour guide rather than regional director of Safety Pins Day Care Center.

"And you're based here in Charlotte?"

"Yes, this is our national headquarters."

Jenners continued. "In your training, do you adhere to any of the recommendations sponsored by the American Academy of Pediatrics?"

"We do," she intoned curtly. "As a matter of fact, an entire training session is devoted to the study of their manual on child care. It is a requirement that each candidate be tested on this material."

Jenners had no further questions.

Elizabeth rose quickly, smoothing invisible wrinkles from her Liz Claiborne dress. "Miss Robertson, you stated that an entire training session is devoted to the recommendations of the American Academy of Pediatrics." Elizabeth acted impressed. "A whole session. You must really be a staunch devotee of the AAPs' standards?"

"They are, if you didn't know, the leading authorities."

"I'm impressed. It's not many in your field who are so patently devoted to classroom participation. And you say you devote a whole, entire session to this line of study. That's amazing."

"Frankly, we're not in the business of producing amazement. We leave that to Disneyland. What we do, quite professionally, is to stimulate your child's sense of awareness so that if he did travel to Disneyland, he would perceive exactly what was taking place rather than being amazed because he is a dimwit fooled by the color and pageantry."

"All this and safety too," Elizabeth commented flatly.

"That's just the minimum of what we do at Safety Pins."

"That's quite a ringing endorsement, Miss Robertson, but I just happened to have a copy of the Safety Pins Child Care Manual." Elizabeth smiled demurely. "There is only one page devoted to the recommendations of The American Academy of Pediatrics. One page," she shrieked. "How is it possible that you could devote an entire class session to such scant information?"

The witness had slightly shifted her position in the witness box. It was if she wanted to be able to see Jenners in case he advised her to plead the 5th Amendment."

"While, Miss Robertson, I don't discount the notion that complete classes were geared toward the study you mentioned, but I also think the actual truth got glossed over in your attempt to conceal just how long a class session is. Most people would assume that an entire class would consume as much time as does a college class, but that isn't true, is it---?"

"Objection!" Jenners leaped to his feet.

"Overruled."

"What's true is that you devote a mere fifteen minutes to a class session. How much learning can take place in that short a time?"

"Well, you see. We---"

Elizabeth patiently waited for her to compose a response. The woman failed.

"Isn't it true that in none of your very short classes is any information provided about CPR?"

"We're getting to that."

"Isn't it true that you only require minimal knowledge of 1st Aid training?"

"There is an upgrade in this area."

"Isn't it further correct that it takes only a minimum of eight hours spread out over a few days to qualify as a day care worker?" Elizabeth sniffed. "It takes 1500 hours to certify as a licensed barber. Before the lady can manicure my nails, she has to complete at least 1500 hours of training and you assume you can produce certified baby-sitters in only six hours?"

It was obvious the jury was incensed. She halted her attack and graciously permitted the witness to breathe. She had no further questions.

So ended the first day of trial.

As expected the first week of trial was bloodless, a soulless parade of experts who either decried or substantiated everything. This was Jenners' scientific circus, a mind-numbing carnival filled with quacks and charlatans who had nothing better to do than publicly address the fact that they didn't know what the hell they were talking about. It seemed that, for the moment, Judge Postman was content to allow Jenners to ring-lead this meaningless charade, camouflaging the necessity to direct a real trial. Everyone knew that Judge Postman was lazy, but this didn't undermine his inherent fairness as long as you kept him attentive. In his golden years, the Judge mainly came to Court to be entertained.

Elizabeth kept that in mind as she rose for her cross-examination.

"Dr. Nelson," she prodded, "you testified under direct examination that over the past decade that a lot has been done to forge better links between children at day care facilities and their care-givers. Explain how this is so?"

Sinclair Nelson, a developmental psychologist at UCLA, spoke in a tone that was slow and sincere. "Much attention has been given to the emotional development of a child in day care. Early on, many individuals felt that day care would be too sterile an environment for healthy emotional bonds to develop normally. Presently, we have learned that this notion is false."

"And this cognitive development is equally as vital in the over-all scheme of things as is, say, cleanliness and safety?'

"Yes, that is true. Mental injury is no less severe than physical injury."

"How then is this fostering achieved, Dr. Nelson?"

"By ideally having your child attended to by the same care-giver."

"Let me interrupt you, doctor, but wasn't there quite a furor over this single caregiver approach not long ago. The debate being that it would be best for a child to have a succession of caregivers as this would be best to prevent the child from bonding too strongly with any one particular caregiver, who could, in fact, come to replace Mommy and Daddy."

"There was, yes, quite a stir over this issue, but it has since been resolved. The younger the child, the more need there is for a single caregiver. This is critical in this attachment phase. It was also realized that the toddler would not come to view the caregiver as a parent, but as a teacher. This insight would be of immense value once the child started school. That is the ideal scenario."

"But not the reality?"

"Far from it. High turnover is primarily responsible." Dr. Nelson grimaced. "Day care is not one of the glamour professions so employees are not highly motivated. As a result, this makes it easier for marginally certified trainees to start work almost immediately."

"So the picture of day care is not rosy due to the level of the caregivers' expertise?"

"Unless caregivers are well-trained, they won't know a cry of hunger from a cry of discomfort. Essentially, day care centers staffed with such people are an accident waiting to happen."

"Thank you, Dr. Nelson. I have no further questions."

Jenners dropped his head in his hands. Elizabeth smiled.

8

By the end of the second week, the shoe was on the other foot. This evening, Elizabeth would start putting on her witnesses.

Jenners was ready.

In essence, his job was easy. Prove everyone liars. He had done it hundreds of times before and he had no intention of not doing it this time. He had to make it somehow appear that her experts had relied on tainted evidence or had used shoddy methods to obtain their accumulated data. Failing this, he would pump the conspiracy theory for all it was worth.

"State your name for the Court". It was Elizabeth speaking.

"Anna Chanel Myerson."

"You work for?"

"The Mecklenburg County Human Resources Services."

"Were you employed there last year?"

"And for the last ten years preceding also."

"At any time during your tenure with Human Resources were you aware of any complaints lodged against the facility known as Safety Pins Day Care Center?"

"Yes. A complaint came in that involved the case of Warren Hill and William Sloan."

"Had there been any complaints prior to this?"

"Yes."

By the end of the hour, Miss Myerson had indicated that Safety Pins had been the victim of two prior complaints prior to the case of Sloan and Hill. Jenners had immediately felt himself thrust upon the ropes, ready to bob and weave, but found there was no need to duck. The filed complaints of Angie Cummings and her son, both now deceased as well as the Taylor complaint had mysteriously disappeared. No mention was made of these "ghost files."

"Those complaints," Jenners asked on cross-examination, "once you got them, why didn't you instantly move to revoke the license of Safety Pins? Isn't that the common routine, the usual practice in such circumstances?"

"Only when the complaint, or complaints, if there is more than one, is severe enough to justify such a sanction."

"Oh, so I see," Jenners enunciated, "those complaints didn't justify revocation?"

"No. They did not."

"Suspension, perhaps?" Jenners offered.

"No."

"Imposition of a fine, maybe?"

"I object, Your Honor," Elizabeth protested. "to this callous line of pandering. Would you make him get to the point?"

"Your Honor, may we approach the bench?" This was Jenners' request.

Elizabeth rose hurriedly from her seat and hastened to the Judge's bench for a heated sidebar conference. She thought to cast a happy smile at Miss Myerson, abandoned and ignored on the stand, to let her know that it was alright and that this interruption had nothing to do with her.

"Your Honor, I beg the privilege of being allowed to draw out every single inference of suspicion and doubt, and fling these vicious barbs as far away from the integrity of my client as possible." Jenners concluded in a stern, half-mocking tone.

"But to what effect, Your Honor," Elizabeth countered, "to browbeat the witness?"

The Judge motioned towards the jury. "Why dwindle down an opportunity," he mused.

Elizabeth stared numbly at the Judge.

"When you're building a house," Judge Postman lectured, "it's better to use a lot of mortar rather than too little. I think I'll allow that."

"But," Elizabeth insisted," it has already been established that the complaints were of a harmless nature."

The Judge was puzzled. "Was that what you intended to demonstrate by introducing this witness, counselor?"

"Of course not, Your Honor."

"Then I can't understand the probative value of her testimony except that it allows Mr. Jenners to play cat and mouse with the fact that there was no reason to penalize Safety Pins on the face of harmless complaints."

"I do reserve the right, Your Honor, to milk this fact," Jenners grinned.

"You Honor," Elizabeth commented," there were other complaints."

The Judge's bushy eyebrows arched. He whispered. "You don't mean to tell me that your witness has perjured herself? She said there were no other complaints on file."

"On file, Your Honor," Elizabeth groaned. "That's the catch-word. The other complaints were serious."

"But if they were not on file, they don't exist legally, now do they, Miss Sellers?"

"What happened to these so-called alluded to files?" The Judge was still whispering conspiratorially.

"They never existed, Your Honor."

"I was speaking to her, counselor," Judge Postman insinuated, smirking at Jenners. "If you don't mind."

"They got misplaced, Your Honor."

"And I guess you were in such a rush to lower the boom on opposing counsel that you didn't go over the nature of this witness's testimony until, say thirty seconds before you put her on the stand."

Elizabeth nodded. "That's about the size of it, Your Honor."

"To prevent a fiasco like this from occurring in the future, I would strongly advise that you stay in contact with your witnesses. Now, back to your places. Counselor," Judge Postman motioned at Jenners. "You may proceed with your previous line of questioning."

"Now, Miss Myerson," Jenners said after apologizing for the delay, "would you please tell the Court what punitive measures were exacted against Safety Pins due to those heinous complaints against them?"

"Nothing."

"*Nothing?*"

"Miss Myerson spoke low. "There was nothing----"

"I'm going to have to ask you to speak a little louder." Jenners glanced at the Judge. "That would be alright, wouldn't it, Your Honor, if the witness raised her voice a notch or two?"

The Judge scowled. He knew that Jenners didn't particularly desire a response. "Speak up," he commanded the witness anyway.

"The nature of the complaint was so...." She searched for a word.

"Trivial,' Jenners provided considerately. Frivolous," he continued. "Stupid?"

"Objection!" Elizabeth shouted. "He's leading the witness."

"Not at all, sir. I'm just playing Webster's dictionary." He glared at Elizabeth. "The unabridged edition."

"Overruled."

Elizabeth huffed. Frustrated.

"Yes, the complaints were...." She stalled again.

The Judge waved Jenners quiet. "Give her a moment, Mr. Webster. Evidently none of your admissions aptly explained the situation." He addressed the witness. "Feel free to use the language you'd use at the water cooler. We're plain folk here." He indicated the jurors. "No need to dazzle us with words that are going to fly over our heads."

"Thank you, Judge."

Jenners was adamant. Impatient. "Isn't it so, Miss Myerson, that the filed complaints weren't worth two cents?"

"Yes", Miss Myerson finally conceded.

"So, there was nothing to reprimand Safety Pins for, now was there?"

"No."

"Essentially, then, Miss Sellers brought you to Court," Jenners said, acknowledging Elizabeth, "to inform the Court that except for some kooks, Safety Pins is a paragon of excellence. Isn't that true? For all practical purposes, Safety Pins has an excellent safety record.?"

"Yes, that is true."

Jenners made himself appear contrite. "You-you look so peaceful now. So calm. You must have really wanted the Court to know this. You seem so relieved." He faced the jury. "I, for one, thank you from the bottom of my heart. Thank you."

Elizabeth blamed herself. She wallowed in her dejection and embarked on a gut-level trip of self-pity. Due to her oversight, Jenners had pumped life into the idea that Safety Pins was a model second home for children. She knew better. The Sloans and the Hills knew better also. Their sons had the scars to prove it. She still had a few more expert witnesses to call to the stand and she understood that the volume of Jenners' attacks would increase. He wanted to do as much damage as possible before she led him into the emotional "human drama" phase of the trial. However if he could continue to pluck concessions from her then he could effectively dilute the final stages of the trial and force the jury's conclusion to a finding that no negligence attended to the injury of "the boys".

In trial, she had made her first blunder. This was

not a mistake or harmless error. Those could be patched over and doctored until their wounds were just superficial. Blunders were not of that sort.

Elizabeth felt uneasy. Many cases had been lost outright simply by the strength of a blunder. She was consumed by the guilt that her blunder was industrial strength. It was a customary rule of thumb in law school to always know the content of your witnesses' testimony. You did this by staying in contact with them, setting up mock trials, telling them what too say. Under no circumstances did you let them lose valuable evidence.

At Howard, she had been cautioned against such a fiasco. The only thing more distressing that this could occur only if she had the task of conducting a direct examination of a hostile witness. She felt no chance of that happening until...... .

"And you don't remember Lou Smith!?" Elizabeth's jaw dropped.

"Lady, how could I remember speaking to him when I've told you that I don't ever recall having met him?"

Robert Wray was a lawyer's worst nightmare. A once friendly witness turned hostile. During the summer, he had been sent out by members of a local chapter of MFSDC, Moms For Safe Day Care. His job had been to demonstrate just how easy it was to start a day care center in Mecklenburg County. This type of activity was going on all across the country and MFSD was spearheading and coordinating the drive, and once the results were tallied, hoped to have enough ammo to press Congress for more stringent start-up measures. If Charlotte was any indication, then little green men from Mars were welcome to apply.

Wray had a two-bedroom apartment. One of the rooms was converted for use as space for the day care. He had no references. No training. Yet when he plunked down the $50 application fee, without any unnecessary delay, his apartment was inspected and approved. All he had to do before "hauling 'em in" was to install a smoke detector and buy a 1st Aid kit. The harried inspector never felt it prudent to see if Wray's apartment had lights or running water. It had neither.

When Elizabeth had sent her investigator, Lou Smith, to solicit Wray's testimony as to the lax regulations, he had readily agreed. Elizabeth had seen no need at the time to secure a sworn deposition. Another blunder. Nothing spoils good testimony as quickly as pocket money.

"Mr. Wray," Elizabeth cajoled, "is there a medical reason for your memory or are you being difficult for no reason at all?"

"Hmmph," Wray snorted in contempt. "Nothing's wrong with my memory. I can remember all the way back to what I was wearing on the very first day I ever went to school."

"And yet you can't remember Lou Smith?" She pointed at the man seated at her table.

"Can't say that I do with him being so plain and all. If I were him and that concerned about being remembered, I'd suggest purple hair and a chicken bone through the nose. By golly, that would get attention."

A murmur of laughter started bubbling up. The Judge's gavel hand twitched. The laughter turned to polite coughing.

Elizabeth almost screamed. "Your Honor, I'm getting nowhere with this witness. I ask that we delay these proceedings until a voir dire hearing can be held to ascertain if this witness has been bribed, threatened or promised something in return for his courtroom demeanor today."

"You mean to tell me," the Judge winced, "that someone would pay for this sort of behavior?"

"You know what I mean, Your Honor." Elizabeth felt embarrassed.

"Your Honor," Jenners said, rising. "I see no need for voir dire." He nodded at the jury. "Why should she want to hide something from them? As patient as these people have been, listening to us so attentively, it would be disrespectful to conduct a hearing outside of their presence." He paused, pointing accusingly at Elizabeth. "Unless Miss Sellers has something to hide."

"We all know better than that, Your Honor." Elizabeth folded her arms across her chest defensively.

"Your Honor, there is no need for a secret meeting. The witness is sworn in and under oath. Let her question him openly about any so-called bribe money she alleges he may have taken. If Miss Sellers is now dedicating her time to slandering the name of our good citizens, then I feel Mr. Wary, at the very least, deserves witnesses."

"Your Honor,' Elizabeth begged, "may we break for a short recess?"

After recess, it didn't get any better.

Wray openly yawned, not covering his mouth. "I never went down to the county licensing office for any reason. For what," he shrugged, yawning again. This time, he partially covered his mouth.

"Did you call?"

"Yeah, I called, but there's a big difference between calling and going somewhere, now ain't it?"

"Do you recall, by any chance," Elizabeth asked, "the content or nature of that conversation, Mr. Wray?"

"Yeah, it's not what I would call a bonafide conversation?"

"Whatever it was, Mr. Wray, would you mind telling the Court about it?"

"Sure," Wray retorted curtly. "No problem." He sat on the edge of the chair as if to impart vital information he wanted everyone present to hear. "It was a sucker call."

"I beg your pardon." This was Elizabeth.

"A sucker call," Wray repeated. "It was a scam. I called to set the sucker up."

From behind her, Elizabeth heard a collective gasp of horror and then the angry patter of busy pens squeaking across writing pads. The media, of a sudden, had found scandal, had finally struck paydirt.

"I was hired by MFSDC and they gave me the cash to set the county up on this bogus day care scam. They rented out this rat hole of an apartment and sent me to file an application to set up a day care center in my home, only it wasn't my home if you get my drift. This place had no lights and the water was turned off."

"But the fact remains, Mr. Wray, that despite the conditions of this rat hole, you were still approved by a certified board examiner."

"Yeah, so what?" Wray gestured. "Maybe the poor guy was getting a commission for every joint he approved. This wasn't exactly an urban version of 'Field of Dreams' you know. Simply 'cause you got approved didn't mean they would come."

Elizabeth stole a peek at her watch. She felt entitled to a last minute reprieve, but there was still time on the clock. She cuddled up inside the silence of her thoughts, hanging a worn smile on her face to give the impression that she was still functioning, and then started swaying side-to-side. She was close to tears.

The jury felt sorry for her.

Behind her, the gallery swayed in time, keeping pace.

Jenners bared his teeth. Triumph.

The Judge had seen it before. Stress. He banged his gavel. "Court is adjourned for today."

She had cracked. There was no other word for it. She had folded. She had heard of it happening, but never had any intimate knowledge of it....until now. She, Elizabeth Sellers, was now officially inscribed as a victim. She could visualize her name in flowing script emblazoned on the black granite lawyer's "Wall of Shame". *Elizabeth Sellers, Esquire.* Next to her name, the date of infamy. *May 14th.*

Elizabeth wondered where she had gone wrong. Robert Wray was slated to have been the fuse to the powder keg. Instead, he had been a damp firecracker. *Worthless.* In review, Wray was supposed to deliver a heavy-handed sledgehammer blow to the county inspectors and to prove how their chicanery exposed countless children to risk in poorly equipped and poorly managed day care facilities.

In this country, 85% of the day care facilities have been deemed inadequate. A county license is no guarantee or standard of safety for as Wray had demonstrated, for a $50 fee practically anyone could acquire accreditation. It takes longer to study for a driver's license. Attend a single session of training---and you're certified. You can't fail. There are no tests.

No wonder the death toll at day care centers climbed each year. Four hundred deaths a year and still growing.....and growing. Yet these facilities still operate with lax regulations.

Without delay, a restaurant would be shut down if someone found a fly in the soup. Hell, when the federal prison in Atlanta got too violent is 1980, it was closed down and all the prisoners packed up and shipped somewhere safer.

What does that say about America!?

Outside the Courtroom, the sky oozed water, a vaporous cross between drizzle and rain. The sun would be truant all morning. At least that's what Larry Sprinkle, the weatherman had said.

It was Friday. 10:00. Court was in session and on the stand was Arthur Hightower, child advocate for the State of North Carolina.

"You see," Hightower stated, "that even when a legitimate, formal complaint is filed, it will ultimately come down to the child's word against an adult's. You can imagine how that turns out. In just about every instance, the benefit of the doubt is awarded to the grown-up."

"So a lot of complaints do not get filed?"

"Many more that we're aware of."

"And why is this, Mr. Hightower?"

"Because many counties refuse to share files with other counties."

"Objection, Your Honor," Jenners interjected. "That calls for speculation on the part of the witness since the files, as he claims, are not shared."

"Sustained."

Elizabeth felt better this morning, but she was still cautious, on guard to prevent a relapse of yesterday's melancholy. She noted Judge Postman kept a watchful eye as she meandered across the courtroom. She also knew that Jenners would be probing, attempting to reopen her wounds.

"That's where parents are wrong," Hightower fumed. "There are no regular inspections. An inspector visits a center when it first opens and that's it unless someone summons them out in response to a complaint. Just last year an audit revealed that less than a third of the statewide centers had received the two mandatory inspections. Some facilities were not even visited once and when the inspectors did get around to showing up, they conducted only an eyeball inspection."

"Which means?"

"They mainly concern themselves with the availability of a 1st Aid kit. A lot of good that will do when a kid falls off a high chair or gets hit by a car."

"What else? There has to be more?"

"Objection." Jenners ejaculated. "She's leading the witness, milking him dry."

The Judge leered at Jenners. "It's her cow, counselor. Remember yours?"

Jenners sat down. He remembered. "Withdrawn," he moaned.

"On these cursory visits, inspectors may check on the toilets to make sure they flush properly or take a peek in the sinks to make sure there is no standing water while at the same time not checking to see if there is a fence around the swimming pool. I find that totally irresponsible."

"Objection," Jenners shouted, jumping to his feet. "I move to strike the witness's answer."

"On what grounds?"

"The personal comments of the witness. How or what he personally feels is totally irrelevant."

Judge Postman tapped his finger on the gavel. "Answer the question," he warned Hightower, "but don't include personal comments such as what you feel. Understand?"

"Yes, Your Honor."

"Continue."

"Is it possible for you," Elizabeth smiled, "to enumerate for the Court some causes of accidents at these facilities without getting too personal?"

"I'll try," Hightower sniffed.

"Your Honor,' Jenners thundered from his seat, "would you issue a warning that the witness try hard?"

"Your objection is noted, counselor. I'm sure my earlier warning will suffice."

"Do I need to repeat my question, Your Honor?" Elizabeth asked.

"Only at the risk of renewing opposing counsel's objection," Judge Postman said wearily.

Elizabeth smiled at Hightower. "You may answer my question."

Hightower stuffed his hands between his legs, tucked inside his crotch and when recognizing this might be construed as lewd, jerked his hands up quickly as though his pants were on fire. The back of his hand smacked hard into the wood rail. Hightower involuntarily yelped in pain, squeezing his right hand closed over the injured left one.

The Judge ordered a short recess. The Marshal hustled Hightower to an office in the back to ascertain the intent of the injury and to see if medical attention would be needed.

Elizabeth went to the bathroom. She wanted to be alone. She felt like crossing her fingers for luck, hoping that this omen was not an unanimous decision of fate to violate and upset the thorough examination she had done thus far. Bad omens, if this was one, were particularly destructive in the latter stages of a trial since the thought of what could happen was so potent a tranquilizer that it numbed you to the point of nonresistance. You just wanted to finish, to get it over with.

As fragile as she was emotionally, she still had to methodically unravel the "oomph" of her trial strategy whose thunderous appeal had been skillfully tinned by Jenners. She had to gather momentum or the jury would need a magnifying glass in order to see the ragged pieces of the case she had attempted to build. It was a task whose explicit difficulty rested upon the stubborn maintenance of her flagging belief in winning. She slammed her tiny fists upon the glistening porcelain wash basin. She was agitated. She felt like quitting.

No Mas.

Wasn't that the ultimate 'cry uncle?'

She bashed her fists against the sink again, but halted. She stared into the mirror, then averted her eyes, casting them onto her hands. They were shaking. And then without notice too herself, her hands were fists, clenched tight. She smashed the mirror.

BAM!

BAM!

BAM!

Then suddenly she was a crumpled heap on the floor, hugging the old radiator, crying. She wailed shamelessly, her dress bunched up in wrinkled folds around her drawn-up knees.

After a few seconds, she attempted to stand, but didn't quite trust her balance. The stinging tears and the ringing in her ears had wreaked havoc upon her equilibrium. She slid back down to the floor, travelling back in time to when she was a little girl. Now, she felt safe. Mommy and Daddy would make all the bad things go away.

And that is how they found her!

9

Someone in a very distant voice was saying something about "proof" and Elizabeth felt compelled to spring up and to object very loudly, but when her eyes opened she recalled she was not in Court. She was somewhere else. A hospital? Perhaps, an insane asylum. Under her brown skin, she blushed. Embarrassed

Then she recognized her parents.

"How you feeling, dear?" her petite, pretty Mother asked.

"Worse than ever before in my life."

Alarmed, the doctor stepped closer to the bed. "What is it exactly that is bothering you?"

Her father, William, a tall and proud man, introduced the two. Dr. John Kennard was an old friend.

She raised on one elbow and noticed the sun. She was confused.

"It's the next day," her father informed her. "Saturday. See." He pointed at the television. "Cartoons."

"You mean I was that exhausted. I must have slept like a log."

"Well," Dr. Kennard offered, "you had a little help."

Elizabeth glanced at her mother.

"They administered a mild sedative."

"I slept for eighteen hours. I wouldn't call that mild." Elizabeth rolled her eyes, falling back against the pillow. She sighed heavily. "How much is work-related and how much is looney?"

Dr. Kennard smiled professionally. "I think I'll leave now."

"What happened to me?" Elizabeth quizzed her parents once the doctor had left.

"Anxiety. Stress. Depression. Take your pick." Her father grimaced. "There is yet no substantial proof of what triggered that reaction."

"That look on your face is frightening me."

"I don't mean to, but Dr. Kennard feels it may be wise if he referred you to some outpatient supervision for a brief period. No hospitalization," her father assured her warmly, "and no more knock-out drugs." William kissed her forehead softly.

"I'm not........."Elizabeth's voice faded to a whisper, "crazy."

"We know that, sweetheart, but the doctor just wants you to go some place where your individual needs can be assessed and a suitable mental health regimen prescribed."

"Good gracious, Mama, it sound like they've already gotten me fitted for a strait-jacket."

"Please, sweetheart, be reasonable. I'm your father, and your mother and I want only the best for you. This is no slim-fast diet we're discussing. It's your mental health and I refuse to allow you to expose yourself to further harm and danger."

"Do you think I'm suicidal, too?"

"It appears that you've merely suffered a panic attack and I would like to get you referred to a reputable managed mental health care company. I hear Green Springs Health Services is one of the best. You can choose your own----"

"Green Springs!?" Elizabeth exploded, looking helplessly at her father. "That sound like a sanitarium too me."

Before either parent could respond, Dr. Kennard re-entered the room, two male interns at his side. Seeing the needle, Elizabeth flew into a rage, rising to meet the approaching interns. Despite her struggling, the hypodermic syringe found its mark.

Sleep.

Two weeks later, Elizabeth was back in Court, the old courthouse a dark smudge under the bright evening sky. She noticed for the first time how it slouched despairingly against the glittering horizon of other wonderfully tall skyscrapers.

When she had left the office, George Bailey had been upset because she had refused to permit him to sit with her at the counselor's table. She felt that such a move would brand her as weak, insinuating that she had to drag in reinforcements to help her fight her battles. Once the word hit the streets, her career would be over. It still might end right here in the old courthouse, but at least she was going to go down swinging.

Inside the courtroom, the gallery slaves were there in even greater numbers. All had returned, bringing friends, to witness the homecoming of Miss Dementia. She deliberately had to force herself to walk slowly and to boldly greet the probing stares of the packed courtroom.

Reaching her table, she buried her head in her briefcase, readying her notes. Looking up, Jenners slid a piece of paper towards her. The writing on the paper read: *"Hope you're feeling better."* Then in large bold print further down on the same page in clear, cursive writing was another message: *"Submit! I will not be easy on you!"*

After a five minute conference with Judge Postman in sidebar, both attorneys upheld their intention to proceed with trial. The Judge's face became flushed. He had hoped that Elizabeth would be amendable to negotiations now. She was not. He would not baby-sit her. Satisfied that he had done his duty, he flashed Jenners a take-no-prisoners glare, then ordered the trial to commence.

Arthur Hightower, the child advocate, was back on the stand once again. It was time for Elizabeth to complete her direct examination.

"Mr. Hightower," Elizabeth cheerfully said, "it has been a while." She displayed a friendly smile. "I know that after so long a delay, you may not be eager to continue, but I beg your indulgence. The last question I asked you, Mr. Hightower, was for you to enumerate for us some of the causes of mishaps that frequently occur at day care centers."

"*Mishaps?!*" Hightower growled, "that's putting it mildly."

"Your Honor," Jenners bellowed, "I feel it may be necessary to caution the witness again in regards to personal interjections."

Hightower still smoldered with righteous indignation. Elizabeth was elated.

"My warning is still valid," Judge Postman commented. "Answer the questions succinctly."

"But, Your Honor," Hightower protested. "May I be heard on this issue?"

The Judge glared at the witness. "There is to be no challenge to the Court on the matters of procedure, but yes, I will hear you."

"Thank you."

"Make your address," Judge Postman commanded.

"Your Honor, I am a child advocate and I love my job not because of the financial rewards. I love my job because I truly love helping children. I find myself hopelessly unable to speak of them especially in cases where there has been injury without becoming emotional and personal. That's like asking me to leave my heart outside on the courtroom doorsteps. That's akin to what the segregationists asked William Lloyd Garrison to do when they ordered him to be moderate in his condemnation of slavery. As Mr. Garrison so eloquently asked, 'how do you ask a mother whose baby has fallen into a fire to moderately extricate the babe from the flames'? What would have happened, Your Honor, if Paul Revere had galloped through the streets of Boston whispering his immortal, 'The British are coming? The British are coming'"

Hightower's face shone with immeasurable pride and fierce commitment. He sat up straight as an arrow and reached into his pocket. He waved a toothbrush in the air, holding it aloft, as though it was a flag of honor. His voice had depth. "I will not moderate. I will not equivocate. I will not be moved a single inch and I will be heard!.....or Your Honor, you can hold me in contempt."

Someone in the packed courtroom clapped. Another responded in kind. Then another. And another until the entire courtroom swelled with applause. The Judge rapped his gavel. The clapping resumed. When it finally did die down of its own accord, the gallery was sent out to recess and the lawyers were summoned to the Judge's chambers

"Who in the hell does he think he is?" Judge Postman howled, his jowls livid. "Using my courtroom to deliver a soap-box oratory. I've got half a mind to throw him and his toothbrush in jail for about ten days. See what tune he'll be singing then, eh? The little wimp has the audacity to challenge me---in my own dag-blamed courtroom."

"Your Honor," Elizabeth began, "I simply feel the matter is being overstated. It's not---"

"Overstated!" the Judge exploded. "How dare you add insult to injury. Overstated. I'll tell you what, Miss Sellers. I want you to march right out of here this instant and personally deliver this message to Mr. Paul-Revere-William-Lloyd-Garrison or just whoever the hell he thinks he is and tell him that I don't intend to tolerate any of this petty insolence."

Elizabeth visibly sagged. "Your Honor, I spoke with Mr. Hightower before coming to your chambers. He sent you a message. He wants you to know that he is sticking to his guns."

"*What?!*"

"There's more," Elizabeth sighed resolutely.

"More," Jenners goaded. "You mean after that.....there's more? My goodness."

"Your Honor," Elizabeth stood, facing the Judge, "if you're going to insist on holding my witness in contempt, then I recommend that you give me a matching sentence."

Judge Postman was incensed. "*What!?*"

"Good grief," Jenners moaned. "Paul Revere and Joan of Arc in the same trial." He pointed to himself. "Who am I? Casper the Ghost. Am I invisible or what?"

"Calm down, counselor," Judge Postman exclaimed. "You can be heard."

"It was my hopes that with this trial moving again, we could sort of get on with it and conclude within a few days. I'd like to remind everyone that I'm in transit and that I would like to get back to California soon."

"This trial will get moving again." Judge Postman remarked softly, "and we'll have Miss Sellers to thank for it. I'll give her another chance to climb down off her high horse and to do as I instructed her earlier, and march right out of here to talk some sense into the head of that witness of hers. We are understood on this point, aren't we, counselor?"

"I'm sorry Your Honor, but I also must stick to my guns. I'll be ready to go to jail as soon as you issue the order."

"So you're going to challenge me on this?"

"Only as far as it pertains to me abandoning my witness. He feels his personal integrity is at issue here. I will not ask him to compromise."

"That is not a good idea, Miss Sellers, as you very well know."

Elizabeth shrugged casually. "Many of the things that made this country what it is started out as bad ideas. I realize that you have nothing to hold me in contempt for, but I assure you that if you insist on jailing my witness, then I will find a reason to go to jail with him. I want to be clear on that."

"And while you're playing this game, what about your obligations to your clients?" Jenners asked. "Have you forgotten them?"

Elizabeth scowled at Jenners. "If they choose, they can pursue other representation. At the moment, my only concern is with Mr. Hightower. Will he be allowed to testify freely or is Judge Postman going to issue a gag order?"

"Okay." Jenners was exasperated. He cast a woeful look at the Judge. "It appears I started this whole mess with my objection, so let's go back to trial. I'll withdraw my objection---anything---to get this trial on its feet again."

There was a sigh of relief from Elizabeth. She was hopeful.

Judge Postman looked tired, but there was still a stern defiance in his eyes. "I don't know about that," he muttered. "I'm not going to allow some out-of-the-blue witness to waltz into my courtroom and knock me off a decision I've entered into the record." He considered the implication of that. He pulled himself out of his easy chair, walked to his desk, stared at some family portraits. "All this talk about Mr. Hightower's personal integrity." He spun around, clutching a youthful portrait of himself. "But who gives a damn about my personal integrity? What does everyone think I am, a piece of rock in a black robe?" He held up the photo. He spoke sternly. "It has been a long way from there to here, but along the way, I have paved the trip with a solid legacy of achievement and I'm not about to be bullied now by any damned body. I'll throw the whole lot of you in jail until hell freezes over before I let myself get bowled over."

"What do we do then?" Jenners asked sadly. "I'm open to suggestions."

"There is a safe way out," The Judge confessed, "and that is for the both of you to come to terms and settle. That would be ideal for everyone, but can the two of you get along with each other long enough to negotiate a settlement?"

Jenners spoke tentatively, looking at Elizabeth carefully. "There are some conflicting interests, Your Honor."

"Such as-----?"

"She wants----."

"My clients want," Elizabeth interrupted. "I simply serve those interests. I want to get this over with as badly as anyone, but my personal integrity would be called into question if I failed to secure what my clients' want."

"Which is?" Judge Postman asked, still holding the portrait.

Jenners butted in. "Her clients," he spat distastefully, "are going to ask that you order Safety Pins boarded up and nailed closed."

Judge Postman scrutinized Elizabeth incredulously. "Even if you did win the case, I don't know if I would be so inclined to issue a ruling closing the facility down."

"It would be our contention, Your Honor, given your fairness and integrity, that you would do so as a matter of conscience."

"Hmmph, you assume a lot, young lady. It's unbelievable. You uphold my integrity as long as you feel it will suit your clients' case and yet you are willing to stomp on it this evening." The Judge was growing angry again. "I very well may hold your witness in contempt and then jail you for personally obstructing justice by directing him to disobey my orders." Satisfied, he nodded his head. "That's how I'll do it. That's precisely how I'll do it and that's exactly what I'll do unless you two decide to settle."

Jenners looked at Elizabeth. She shook her head sadly. They both sighed in resignation.

"Your Honor," Jenners grimaced. "We both are opposed to negotiation."

"That settles it then. I don't want any tears in the end when this is over. Everyone is settled in as a matter of principle. Personally," Judge Postman warned, "I do not intend to be put to shame and ridicule." He glared at both attorneys. "Counselors, make your beds good because you've got to lie in them."

"There is another way, Your Honor," Elizabeth commented blandly.

The men stared at her. Waiting.

"You could remove yourself from the case, Your Honor."

Astonished, Judge Postman's eyes narrowed. Spittle spewed from his lips. "*Remove myself?!* What kind of tomfoolery is that? If anything, Miss Sellers, I should dismiss this case outright and forthwith." He pointed his finger at her, his forbearance completely lost. "I have been overly patient with you and you have come far short of proving anything except you're very skilled at wasting the good money of taxpayers. I will no longer allow you the latitude that I have thus far. In essence, young lady," the Judge raged, "you have just run out of rope." He turned to Jenners. I'm not even going to consider a Motion of Withdrawal of that damned objection from you. I won't strike it, you hear that? It is cast in stone and there is not a thing, legal or otherwise, that either of you can do about it." He strode to the door of his chambers. "This is what is going to transpire out there in open court. I will commence the proceedings and once your witness, Miss Sellers, is back on the stand, I am going to direct him to answers questions in compliance with my earlier order which I will issue again. If he refuses, then his ass is going to jail, but not before I ask you, Miss Sellers to personally counsel and direct your witness to comply with an order of the Court and if you refuse to do so, then," he sighed, "it's off to jail for your ass too!"

He snatched open the door.

"I'll see you in Court, counselors!"

GESTAPO JUDGE, the sign read.

Another screamed: **DELIVER THE POSTMAN TO JAIL!**

There were others. Lots of them.

Lou Smith dipped his massive shoulders as he cut through the thong of marching picketers outside the front entrance of the jail and entered the ground level reception area. He hurried to the glass-paneled security booth and pushed his driver's license under the opening at the bottom of the counter.

The deputy stared at the smiling chocolate face on the plastic, picked up the phone and mumbled into the receiver. After nodding her head vigorously a few times, she re-cradled the phone and returned the driver's license. She used her head to point out the general direction of the elevator.

"Punch Four."

On the fourth floor, the elevator opened onto a narrow, brightly-lit hallway across from a bank of visiting booths. On his side there was no door, simply a bricked-in stall facing a thick slab of security glass. On the other side of the shatter-proof glass, the prisoner's side, was a room. Unlike his cubicle, that side had a door that undoubtedly would be slammed shut and locked once the prisoner arrived.

A guard got his attention and waved him towards the Sergeant's desk which was nestled into a divider that separated the attorneys' booth from the personal visitors' booth.

The Sergeant on duty, a burly, black man with salt and pepper hair recognized Lou. "Hey, you that investigator of that lady lawyer, ain't you?"

Lou nodded.

"Yeah, I thought so. Caught you on the news with her a few times. That's fucked up what that cracker Judge did to her, man."

"Tell me about it" Lou groaned.

"Since you a private investigator, tell you what I'm gonna do. I'll let you visit in the attorney's booth. More privacy. I'm getting ready to leave and my replacement is a jack-ass."

"He can't cause problems in the booth, can he?"

"No, but he can be nosy as hell. The booths are monitored on the family side and some of these assholes will monitor your conversation if they feel they might pick up some juicy gossip. With all the shit your lady friend in, some bastard would have the tape running, hoping to catch a story to tell the Captain about or to sell to the newspapers. On this side", he pointed to the lawyer's booth, "they don't fuck around." The Sergeant grinned. "This side got that lawyer/client confidentiality shit going on for it. Go on down. I'll get your lady friend up here in a minute."

A few minutes, Lou saw Elizabeth's face peering through the square window in the door, looking for him. She stepped inside the room and the door was locked closed behind her. She rushed to the front of the booth and pasted her small hand, outstretched, onto the thick, dirty glass. Lou did the same.

"I have some good news, Miss Sellers. You're getting out of this dump today."

"What about Mr. Hightower?"

"Him too."

"How did you mange that?' Elizabeth gushed. "It's just been three days. The Judge gave us ten."

"The dudes at your firm got another judge to rescind the order. Postman is off the case."

"Thank God," Elizabeth prayed. "Who's on?"

"Tom Williams. He's fair. You'll like him." Lou shook his head. "You won't believe the kind of publicity this issue has generated and the picketers have simply been unbelievable. They have come out in droves every day. They picket here at the jail and up at the federal courthouse. You have your old friend, Sandra, to thank-
-."

"*Sandra?!*" Elizabeth screamed. "*Sandra from school!?*"

Lou nodded.

"She's here?!"

"She's here."

Elizabeth screamed again.

Lou smiled. "Better hurry up and get you out of here before you go stir crazy." He saluted and left.

10

Judge Thomas Williams revered adoption. Children. Cats. But not hand-me-down cases from other judges. These orphans had a disarming manner of squirming their way into your life, baby-powdered with innocence to disguise their stink, and then maturing into full-blown chaos. He didn't care for them at all. Too him, they were so very much like stepping into someone else's shit.

Now, all of a sudden he had to baby-sit one.

Tom Williams was an enigma among black judges in the south. He presided over civil trials, cases pertaining to personal injury and medical malpractice suits rather than the more noteworthy, headline-grabbing criminal trials with shady characters where it was often difficult to distinguish the good guys from the bad guys.

Despite the fact that he was unassuming and modest, he had done well. He had graduated Harvard with honors which had made his path smooth with the guilt of blood money and muted tokenism.

In those early days, white folk had grudgingly fawned over him, inspired or intimidated by the brilliant depth of his mind. From this quarter, applause and accolades. From another quarter, he was booed and hooted at, viewed as a lap-dog. Men of color, his brethren, became his proud adversaries, demonizing him in print and slandering the authenticity of his achievements. They shouted that he was a made man. Hell yes, he would shout back. "I made the excellent grades. I made the money. I made it out of the reach of Jim Crow."

And then they would be still.

But he had gotten away with so much. He had married white twice in an age when blacks such as Emmit Till had gotten lynched just for daring to cast dark eyes upon the pristine beauty of a southern belle. Yet they had allowed him to sleep openly in holy, legal matrimony with them, pump half-breed children out of them, and when mood dictated to slap them around. Oh what privilege they accorded him. And he was as dark as sin.

Birthdays---sixty-five of them---had conferred upon him an aged countenance, and he wore his wisdom in his eyes. His thick, African features, broad nose, thick lips, well-oiled by a million smiles, were regaled with stark handsomeness. His good looks were of the sort that even nature wanted to preserve them, so despite his growing old, his historic beauty was left unmarred.

Inside his chambers, Tom Williams stood and kicked the kinks out of his legs. It was almost time for Court to commence. He had studied the case carefully. He would be machine-like fair. He would baptize this case with the fire of calm, legal restraint, marrying it to sound precedent and honeymooning it to a satisfying climax. It was his call. It was his Court. And it was now ten o'clock.

Time to get cracking.

He had been asked the same thing twice before, but this time when Elizabeth posed it, Arthur Hightower didn't flinch.

"Yes," he stated, "I would like to enumerate some of the causes of accidents at day care centers. The most prevalent oft-repeated ones are drowning, SIDS, faulty playground equipment, falls, being hit by cars."

"So being hit by a car is not a rare, isolated incident?"

"No. It is quite usual."

"Why, Mr. Hightower, do you suppose that is?'

"Greed, mainly. Day care centers are profit-oriented institutions and in many instances, they will pack the children in, thereby ignoring the proper child/adult ratio. That is a violation of the law. In addition to the reported accidents, there are frequently more terrifying accidents that are hushed up and kept quiet."

"Such as?" Elizabeth prodded.

For a full twenty minutes, Hightower vented his anger against the lax regulations of day care centers. Elizabeth put him through his paces and he followed her leads smoothly. He spoke strongly, convincingly, his sentences composed of a pyramid of words that visibly affected the jury. His voice played well with the acoustics of the old courtroom and by the time he had finished even Judge Williams had sagged in his chair, feeling sorry for the children.

Only Jenners was unmoved. In the end he rose, fiddling with his silk necktie. He even smiled at Hightower. Jenners stood in the well of the courtroom and then turned slowly in a complete circle as if searching for a hideout. "Why, Mr. Hightower," he said softly, "I'm surprised at you. You have spent all morning on the stand and not once did you mention all the money you're going to get soon."

Elizabeth was on her feet. She said nothing.

Hightower fumed. "*What money?* I have no idea what you're talking about?"

"There's no need to be modest, Mr. Hightower. You can tell us all about it. You've told us everything else."

"*Objection!*" Elizabeth shouted. "I think that counsel should be reprimanded if he is implying that Mr. Hightower was or will be remunerated for his testimony."

"Counselor?" Judge Williams thundered, looking at Jenners, questioning him with his eyes.

"That's not my point at all, Your Honor. May I proceed? I'm sure the Court will acknowledge the relevance of this line of questioning."

"Very well, then. Proceed."

"You are going to be rich soon, aren't you, Mr. Hightower?"

"How so?"

Jenners acted both surprised and shocked. "You did sue Judge Postman, didn't you?"

Now it was Hightower's turn. Surprise. Shock. "Sue Judge Postman? Whatever for?"

"The injury, Mr. Hightower. Remember the injury to your hand?"

"The Judge had nothing to do with that. Why would I even think of suing him?"

"Well, it happened in his courtroom."

Hightower was incredulous. "But that was an accident."

"Yes, I understand that, Mr. Hightower," Jenners taunted, "but wasn't Judge Postman negligent?"

Elizabeth stared in horror. She knew where this was headed. So did the Judge. So did the VIPs. The Others. The jury. Only Hightower didn't know.

"Of course, not. Why should the Judge be negligent for an accident I caused myself?"

"Then why, pray tell, should a day care center be held liable in the exact same set of circumstances?"

Hightower now got it. He knew. He fussed, fumed, tried to say something.

"I have no further need of this witness, Your Honor," Jenners said curtly. He turned, smiled at Elizabeth. "Thank you," he said soundlessly.

The scientific phase of the trial had lasted for over a month and Jenners had not been either surprised or dismayed by the results. Both lawyers still stood in the middle of the road. That, to Jenners was good. He had not gotten left behind and hadn't surrendered an inch of ground he had gained. Good. Very good.

But now, he carefully assessed the situation before him. The human drama part of the trial was set to begin immediately. He measured the odds against him and decided he could still win. He knew that Elizabeth would seek to draw out every painful detail of the injuries and he knew it would be difficult for him to win points with the jury during cross-examination. He would just have to be content with controlling the amount of damage she did when she put the boys on the stand.

He had not heard from the Senator since the trial commenced, but he realized that Gaylord was well aware of everything that had gone down. Every gain. Every setback. They all had been precisely calculated, laid out side-by-side, examined. Without a doubt, the Senator knew exactly how things stood.

He turned his attention away from Gaylord and instantly his thoughts were occupied by the emotions that would be unearthed by the tears of Tamara Sloan and Deborah Hill. Tears were a powerful inducement for sympathy and juries tended to vote with their hearts instead of their heads. Make 'em cry and win their vote.

Finally, he focused on Elizabeth

Jail had been therapeutic for Elizabeth. Not spa-like therapeutic, but it had helped her focus. Deprivation has a way of making things clearer, sharper. It was almost as if someone had perched zoom lens on her nose like a pair of granny glasses. There wasn't much she missed. Even when she ate a morsel of chocolate, her taste buds greedily sought out all the subtle nuances and textures of the various blends of cocoa that defined the candy. She was able to discern every sensual calorie that comprised that morsel. That's how alert and alive she was to everything.

In her office, she had just completed her trial rehearsals with both Deborah Hill and Tamara Sloan.

They were primed. Now, all she had to do was to bring the show before a live audience. Neither of the women was particularly shy so they would not be intimidated by the crowd, but the passive gallery was never much a major concern. Hilton Jenners III was. He was the gist of anything that could possibly go wrong. The man was like a dysfunctional monster from a recurring nightmare. The only way to successfully contend with him was to be wide awake and on your toes.

She was delighted to be headed back to Court with the momentum rolling in her favor. Now, she had solid evidence, testimony that opposing counsel couldn't squeeze concessions from or cast doubt upon. Scientific evidence was open to debate and could so easily be explained away or reduced to nothing. Emotional testimony could not be so easily bartered away or whittled down.

Elizabeth persuaded herself to think positive and then spent the next hour listening to Jennifer Hudson.

She was going to win.

"Tamara Sloan," the woman said.

"And do you reside in Charlotte?"

"I do,"

Elizabeth appeared interested. "Do you have children?"

"Yes. A son."

"I understand that you work outside the home."

"I do."

"Then how is it possible," Elizabeth asked, "to work and care for your son?'

"William attended day care," Tamara started. "Or at least he did."

"Umm," Elizabeth pouted. "Did something happen to make you remove your son from day care?"

"Yes," Tamara retorted, "it sure did."

"Before we get to that incident, Miss Sloan, could you tell us the name of the day care center?"

"Safety Pins Day Care Center."

"And that's here in Charlotte?"

"Yes."

"Safety Pins is fairly new in Charlotte. How did you come to choose it?"

"I was approached---"

"Objection!" Jenners howled. "Irrelevant and has no bearing on outcome. It was she who decided to place her child in the day care."

"Sustained."

"Did you feel initially that Safety Pins was safe?"

"Objection!" Jenners yelped. "The question has no merit considering the fact that Miss Sloan did place her child in that particular facility---unless Miss Sloan deliberately planted her son there."

Elizabeth saw the trap. "Withdrawn, Your Honor," she responded.

"Move to strike," Judge Williams intoned.

Elizabeth glared annoyingly at Jenners.

He glared back.

'What kind of facility was Safety Pins?"

"Well, I admit it was clean and new. That impressed me."

"What about staff? Did you get the chance to speak with personnel?"

"They were friendly enough."

"But friendliness doesn't always amount to competence, does it?"

"Objection, Your Honor. That calls for a conclusion on the part of the witness that she is not qualified to make."

"Sustained."

This time the glaring was done by Judge Williams. Elizabeth was the target.

The more she thought about it, the more she drilled for personal information intending to portray William as young and healthy. She paid careful attention as she watched the case build inside her head. Time after time Jenners attempted to disrupt her rhythm with his ceaseless objections, but now that she possessed it, she would not relinquish it. *Rhythm.*

"And now, Miss Sloan, would you detail for the court the incident that made you personally aware of Safety Pins' negligence?"

"My son was injured."

"You mean William?"

Jenners stood. "Your Honor, I object to the unnecessary dramatics. It is clear to the Court that the witness meant William since he is her only son."

"What is it that you are suggesting, counselor?"

"That Miss Sellers be asked to conduct her examination in a more sobering fashion."

"Is that all, counselor?"

"At this time, yes, Your Honor."

Judge Williams looked at Elizabeth. "Miss Sellers," he said sternly, "carry on."

Elizabeth caught the growing smile in time, detoured it by pressing her lips together. "You may answer my question, Miss Sloan."

Before Tamara could speak, Jenners was up again. Elizabeth stomped her foot angrily.

"Your Honor, I would, at this point, have my objection noted in the record as I feel Miss Sellers will not desist from a pointedly patronizing vein of examination."

"Object, then, counselor."

Objection!" Jenners hollered loudly.

"Noted," Judge Williams muttered softly. "Now, let's move along." He directed the witness to answer the question.

At any moment, Jenners knew the floodgates would be opened and since he was not anxious to force an issue that would cause the Judge to hold a grudge against him later, he took a seat. He immediately contemplated the quiet authority of the witness and without delay pieced together the appropriate course of action. He couldn't wait to cross-examine her. He'd see how long the tears lasted then.

"I did as I always do---"

"Let me interrupt you for a second if you don't mind," Elizabeth begged. "I forgot to ask you something. Was William healthy when you left home on the morning in question?"

"Yes, he was."

"You didn't have a wreck or anything on your way to dropping your son off, did you?"

"No."

Elizabeth assumed a posture of benign contrition. She sighed deeply, playing to the jury. "As much as I hate to, Miss Sloan, I must ask this question." She walked away from the witness stand so that she would have to speak louder. "Now, Miss Sloan, from the time you left your home until the moment you arrived at Safety Pins, did you or did you not beat your son?"

The blunt question took Tamara by surprise. She wasn't expecting it.

"Hell no, I didn't beat my son."

Elizabeth nodded her head. The almost too perfect answer.

"Objection!" Jenners shouted.

"To what?" the Judge asked.

"The language."

"That's my job, thank you," the Judge scolded. He said nothing to Tamara.

"Remembering that you're under oath, are you telling this court that when you dropped your son off at day care that morning he was healthy and well?"

"Yes, that's exactly what I'm saying."

"After you dropped him off, what then?"

"I went to work."

"What time did you return?"

"4:45 that same evening."

"What happened then, please?"

"I went into the receptionist's office to sign William out and Miss Phillips asked me to wait, that Mr. Tanner, the Director was there and needed to see me. I thought that William had been cutting up or something like that. I had no idea he had been hit by a car."

"*What?!* Elizabeth exploded. "*Hit by a car!?*"

The gallery gasped. The jury sucked in it's breath.

"Yes, hit by a car. Run over."

"Where were day care personnel?"

"Not looking after my son, that's for sure."

"What did they tell you had happened to your son? How did they explain it?"

Tamara smirked. Contempt dripped from her lips. "These folks were so incompetent they didn't even know my son had been hit. They told me he was missing from the premises and that they didn't know where he was."

"And just where was your son, Miss Sloan?"

"In the hospital. In traction. I found out about it on the news that evening."

"*What!?*" It was Elizabeth. Play-acting again.

This time the jury gasped. Even louder than the VIPs. The Others.

"So, the complete time they had you under the impression that William was missing, he was in the hospital...in critical condition...undergoing surgery?"

"That's right." Tamara moaned, dabbing her eyes. "I had to find out on the television that my son had almost been killed." Tamara broke down and cried.

The Judge instantly convened for a fifteen minute recess.

Elizabeth paced nervously, glancing every few seconds at her watch. She didn't want to give the jury the benefit of a break. She would rather have continued her examination unabated. Anyway, the foundation was now laid. All that had to be done now for her to advance the theory of negligence was to keep plugging away at Tamara and then Deborah, tugging at the heartstrings. She intended to Xerox the image of "the boys" into the emotional breastplate of each juror and transform the duo into a symbol as heartbreakingly painful as the Easter seal poster child. The image of that was always agonizing.

She counted on her fingers while talking softly too herself about other issues she wanted to raise after she was sure the jury had been branded with more than enough evidence to render a verdict favorable to her clients.

So far Jenners had posed no threat, but as long as he was present in the courtroom, he was a danger. He was slightly wounded, but she knew he was not the type of animal to stop and to lick his wounds. Instead, he would keep on coming---faster---until you took him out of his misery....or until he destroyed you.

Elizabeth knew what time it was. DO or DIE!

"Now, Miss Sloan," Elizabeth resumed after the break. "You mentioned that you found out about your son on the news. Why would Safety Pins deny you such knowledge of your son's whereabouts? I find that especially cruel. I find that totally reprehensible. The news. Did they, for a fact, know where your son was?"

"They absolutely did not." Tamara sobbed. "Even after the accident, the lady in charge still didn't know that my son was missing."

"*They didn't!*"

"No, which goes to prove they don't keep up with their children. The accident happened around lunchtime and then some five hours later, this bitch---excuse me---woman was still under the impression that William and his friend were accounted for."

This was another defining moment for Elizabeth.

Elizabeth shrieked. "You mean there was another child involved?"

The jury moved to the edge of their chairs. Alert. Anxious. Waiting.

"Yes."

The jury frowned.

"Was he run over by a car as well?"

"Yes, he was."

The jurors flopped back in their seats. Three faces registered shock. Two faces exhibited amazement. Five faces, two men, three women, showed disbelief. The remaining two faces were stunned and one of these faces belonged to a man who looked ready to kill.

"While I can't imagine losing account of one child under your care, the complete loss of two is unbelievable. That's neglect magnified a thousand times."

"Objection!" Jenners screamed. "She's inflaming the jury."

"Overruled."

"Don't you feel that your son and his friend were neglected?"

"Sure, that's how I feel. How do you let children just wander off unsupervised and what makes it so bad is that this happened at sleep time. It should have appeared that two cots were empty. She must have left the room, leaving the children unattended."

"I object, Your Honor. That calls for speculation on the part of the witness."

"Sustained."

Jenners took his seat.

Elizabeth paced, thinking. *How do I get the bitch out of the room?*

"Well, then, Miss Sloan, if your son was supposed to be taking a nap," Elizabeth quickly glanced at Jenners, "since that is what they do a slumber time, how could he get hit?"

"The woman obviously left the room and while she was gone, the boys wandered off."

Elizabeth grinned triumphantly. She wanted to wink her eye at Tamara, but resisted the impulse. "But still, how could they have gotten out? All doors and exits should have been secured."

"Objection!". It was Jenners. "Purely speculative."

"No, it isn't, Your Honor. She can relate what information the incident report contained."

"Objection, Your Honor. That would amount to hearsay."

"Not if it came directly from Miss Lassiter herself," Elizabeth countered. "The report is her evidence so it's not hearsay."

"Your Honor," Jenners intoned solemnly, "I would move to strike any such testimony revealed from such sources and ask that you instruct the jury to disregard it. As a matter of fair play, counsel should have alerted me to the existence of any existing documents that purport to be an admission on behalf of anyone employed by my client."

"Such documentation, as I have always understood it, is a matter of public record. I'm sorry, counselor, but there's no smoking gun." Judge Williams smirked. "There's only your failure to do a thorough sweep to locate and secure all material facts pertaining to this case. I don't see where Miss Sellers has breached any principle of law or committed anything underhanded, so if you still choose to object, Mr. Jenners, go right ahead. Be my guest."

"I object, Your Honor."

"Even before the testimony is rendered," Judge Williams chuckled.

"Your Honor, I object that the elicited testimony is to be extracted from inadmissible evidence."

"Overruled.

"Answer the question, Miss Sloan," Elizabeth offered.

"Miss Lassiter---"

"*Objection!*"

"Told investigators that---"

"*Objection!*"

Judge Williams refused to strike the testimony.

"She had put all the children---"

"Objection, Your Honor. Move to strike."

Judge Williams banged his gavel and spoke with heated indignation. "You are beginning to tread in dangerous waters, counselor. While I may recognize your position, I point out that it is a needless one. You are fortunate that I have maintained a distance from your pointless disruptions without reprimand. Your objections are duly recorded and are in fact a matter of record."

"B-but, Your Honor," Jenners stammered.

"I wish to be clear on this. No more senseless and futile objections. All others I will gladly entertain." He turned to Tamara. "Please continue."

"Miss Lassiter said---"

"No," the Judge corrected, "if you read that, then Miss Lassiter didn't say anything, did she?"

Tamara sighed. She was beginning to tire. "Miss Lassiter...." She searched for a word.

"*Reported.*" Help from one of the reporters.

"Reported," Tamara resumed, "that once the children were on their mats that she opened the locked exit door and then left the room to cut off the air conditioner. It was probably during this time that the children walked off. The door was wide open."

"Objection! Speculation on the part of the witness," Jenners declared. "She has no way of knowing if this is when or how the children left."

"Sustained."

"Didn't Miss Lassiter get questioned by a police officer immediately after the accident?" Elizabeth inquired.

"According to the report, a CMPD officer approached the day care center."

"Why would he do that?"

"No one in the neighborhood knew who the children were so the officer felt they might have attended the day care. When he asked Miss Lassiter, she told him that all her children were safe and accounted for."

"And she still hadn't noticed the two empty mats?"

"Evidently not."

"Was there anything in the notes that suggested that Miss Lassiter, as a precaution, took a head count to insure precisely that none of her children were missing?"

"No, nothing in the report indicates that she did any such thing. Even though, there had been a terrible accident and she had left the children unattended in a room with an open door that should have been locked, she took no precautions, none whatsoever, to insure that my son and the others were safe. She went right on about her business while my son was lying in the streets almost dead." Tamara burst into tears. "That bitch was negligent."

Another recess was called. Time for lunch.

As always, at recess, Elizabeth began a tour of the lavatory, pacing quietly back and forth, up and down the narrow, paint-chipped stalls, thinking almost aloud. Out of a small crack of a window cut into a jagged square over the ancient coil radiator, she was able to see Old Betsy, the flag, swaying in the breeze. She could also view the entourage of jurors leaving the courthouse. She studied them, trying to decipher where the seat of power rested, but could discern nothing. They moved as one. No one stood out.

Elizabeth thought of Judge Williams, trying to discover if she felt any special judicial relationship with him because they were people of color. She did not. From him, she would get no more than the customary, unspoken acknowledgement of the wounds he knew she had suffered to get here---from there. So far he had acted by rote, neither to the left nor right of any emotions he might have. He was Spock in black robes. Vulcan-like cold. Logical. Her case was not about to crumble him.

As soon as she finished presenting her witnesses, she would instantly move for a directed verdict. What would this do? The law was clear that the evidence must be viewed in a light most favorable to the plaintiffs and from what he had heard thus far, a ruling in her favor should be granted. She laughed. He would never do it. He would send the case to the jury. That was safe, even for Spock, the Vulcan.

Recess would soon be over.

The ugly glare of every eye in the courtroom made the hair on the back of Jenners' neck bristle. He treaded through the funereal haze to within inches of the witness stand and then abruptly went back to his counsel table. He rummaged inside his briefcase.

Within those scant seconds away from the relative security of the counsel's table, he had been perceptively successful at monitoring the mood of the jury. Somber, overall. Too him, individually---threatening.

The remainder of Tamara Sloan's testimony had been emotion-wracked, a HBO tear-jerker. She had spoken with genuine pain, with hurt so raw and real that there was no need for guise or embellishment. With an aggressive voice, tempered with the maternal love of a mother for her child, she had, with sincerity as warm as breast milk, turned Safety Pins, his client, into a living, breathing monster.

Damned Gaylord.

"Miss Sloan," he began, "you don't know how or when you son left the safety of the facility, do you?"

"What difference does it make?" Tamara snapped. "He left and he got hit by a car."

Jenners smiled tightly. "It's important too me and it's only fair to the jury that they receive all the facts. Now, in Miss Lassiter's well-known report, she didn't lie. She honestly admitted she had opened the door and stepped out of the room briefly, didn't she?"

"Yes...And?"

"But did she say that that was when the two little boys left?"

"When else could it have been?"

"But Miss Lassiter didn't say that."

"She didn't know when they left."

"Aha," Jenners deduced quietly. "You're right. She didn't know. Maybe the reason Miss Lassiter did not notice the two empty mats at slumber time was because there were no empty mats. Suppose that the children had already sneaked away before slumber time? That may account for the reason why Miss Lassiter told the officer all her kids were accounted for. Maybe all the ones she had laid down sleeping mats for were all still there....accounted for." He walked close to Tamara. "When you drop William off, what is the first thing you do?"

"I sign him in."

"You sign him in," Jenners mused, chewing on this information. "And while you're in the act of signing him in, what does William do?"

"He hangs up his book bag and then joins the other kids."

"In other words, Miss Sloan, he leaves you?"

"Yes, that's right."

"What if, on that morning, William didn't join the other children? What if your son walked right back out of the door?"

"I. He---"

"Precisely, Miss Sloan. Your son could have very well marched himself back out of the door that you opened coming in. Isn't it a possibility that in the very brief interval while you were signing William in and the actual moment the facility became legally responsible for his safety could have very well been the second it took for your son to disappear? Maybe you were negligent."

"Objection!" Elizabeth shouted. "There's nothing in the evidence to support this."

"That's what I'm trying to establish, Your Honor."

"Overruled."

"I just happened to stop in at Safety Pins and I had a look at the receiving door. A big heavy door, isn't it, Miss Sloan?"

"Yes, so what?"

"Probably nothing," Jenners maintained, "but while I was there, I just happened to notice that on the door were printed words. Do you recall what those words are, Miss Sloan?"

"Can't say that I do," Tamara blurted.

"Ahh yes, the human mind—marvel that it is---will sometimes let you forget something important. At any rate, the words were....wait; let me think because I want to get them all right. Ah, yes," he said. I remember the words. They read: **PLEASE CLOSE DOOR BEHIND YOU!** You see, if you don't pull the door closed behind you tightly", he gestured, "the door won't shut. It appears the building contractors made a boo-boo. Believe me, they did. I didn't do what the writing commanded me to do and each time that ol' darn door just wouldn't close. Isn't that something? Now, this is what your lawyer would call relevant so listen up. Did you do what the writing on the door ordered you to do that morning, Miss Sloan?"

Silence.

"DID YOU OR DID YOU NOT, MISS SLOAN?!" Jenners boomed. "It's a rather simple question."

Still. Silence.

Tamara fidgeted. Squirmed.

"You don't remember, do you, Miss Sloan?" Jenners said softly, offering her a way out.

"No," Tamara groaned. "I don't remember."

Jenners flung his body around as if he had been suddenly been possessed by an evil spirit. *"She doesn't remember."* He slapped himself upside the head loudly. "Unbelievable. She doesn't remember." He faced Tamara accusingly. "From your earlier testimony, you made it appear as if you are Claire Huxtable, the premier Mama. Let me ask you this, then, Miss Sloan." He chuckled.

"When you go to McDonald's and buy little William a Happy Meal, don't you read the words on the package the toy came in. These words are a warning of safety because they instruct you that the contents may contain small parts that could be swallowed by a small child. These are good words, made up for the safety of your babies." He paused. "Now, when your little William gets sick and the smart doctor slaps the instructions on the medicine bottle, you wouldn't forget to follow what those words say, now would you, Miss Sloan?"

"No, of course, not."

"Of course, you wouldn't. You know why? Because you know those words are there to protect your child. They are there for your child's safety and if you love your child, there is no way you would ignore those words or at any time not remember to follow them. You do love your son, don't you?"

"YES!" Tamara screamed. "YES."

"Then, why," Jenners said patiently, "would you ignore the safety label on that ol' darn door? By ignoring that warning, I contend that you were negligent. You made two very potentially dangerous mistakes that morning. First, you left a door wide open that should have been closed and second you let your son out of your sight before he became the official property of Safety Pins. It could very well be that you're liable for the accident of your son."

The entire courtroom was enthralled, listening attentively. Like a skilled magician, Jenners had made the jury's anger disappear. With sleight-of-hand, he had transferred the crux of the trial from the heart to the head. Elizabeth had gotten to their hearts. He had gone to their heads. He didn't want them feeling. He wanted them thinking.....What if?

Jenners pressed on. "It is very conceivable that the moment you took your eyes off him, to let him have a little space, that it was this exact moment that William slipped out of the door, Miss Sloan. *The door you had left open*! That ol' darn door with those good words on it." He pretended he was finished, began to walk away, stopped. Turned. And stared. "I know you have a problem remembering things," he suggested, lightly tapping his head. "That ol' human mind. Anyway, tell us something. It may not actually make any difference to anyone else in this courtroom or possibly in all of this great metropolitan area, so I just ask you to tell me. When little William got hit, did he have his coat on?"

Tamara frowned, snarling. "Yes, he had his coat on."

"Isn't it funny? If William left the day care during slumber-time when he was supposed to be sleeping, what was he doing with his coat on? Seems like he would have taken it off. You know what I think, Miss Sloan? William never took his coat off that morning. He may have intended to, but when he saw that door open, the same one you had left open, he marched right back outside. Lord knows where he went or what he did all morning, but you set him up. Yes, your only son got hit by a car, but it was your negligence that caused it."

The jury. The VIPs. The Others. They all gasped as one.

Court was adjourned for the day.

****

Once completed, Deborah Hill's testimony was a reasonable facsimile of Tamara Sloan's. A two-hanky tear-jerker. Jenners winced. The narrow margin of plausibility he had painstakingly eked out had been vastly disturbed by Elizabeth's typical reversal of the thought process. Once more, the thinking was heartfelt, bathed in tears. He simply would have to put on an encore performance, but could he sway they jury as he had yesterday. For almost anyone else, it would have amounted to an exercise in futility, an insurmountable challenge, but he was not merely anyone else. He was Hilton Jenners III and that made all the difference in the world.

He fingered his gold, silk tie lovingly and then rose to begin his cross-examination of the witness, Deborah Hill.

"And Miss Hill, did you suspect anything at all when you arrived at the day care center and saw Miss Sloan standing outside the reception area weeping?"

"No, not in relation to my son. To tell the truth I didn't really think it could have anything to do with any of the children there."

"And why was that?'

"I mean, well, I-I just thought the place was safe." Deborah sighed. "I was wrong, though. The place wasn't safe."

"What were you told at that point?"

"Two officers informed me that my son was missing."

"That's what they said, missing? Not that your son had been hit by a car?"

"That's what they might have said, but it wasn't what happened. My son had been hit. And that's a fact."

"A fact is a fact is a fact," Jenners chanted absently. He went to his table and shuffled through a stack of papers. He spoke over his shoulders. "What made the CMPD believe that your son was missing?"

"Because they're stupid."

The VIPs were silent. Half of the Others laughed.

"Oh yes," Jenners mused, "the perils of police stupidity. Almost as bad as their brutality." At last he found what he had been searching for. "I see from this sign-out sheet, that it was not uncommon for your son's father to pick Warren up from day care." He stood in front of the witness stand and gently released the single sheet of paper. It fluttered like a feather, dropping neatly in Deborah's lap. "Do you recognize that as a copy of the sign-out sheet used at Safety Pins?"

"Yes." Deborah spoke with certitude. "What about it?"

"Read over that for a second and then tell me if you see Warren's father name on the log as the designated pick-up person."

"That's a fact and his name is on here quite a few times." She pursed her lips. "I knew you would want to know how many times, so quite a few times should suffice as an answer."

Jenners turned, facing the jury, a look of sheer appreciation on his face. "She *helped me*," he gushed. "*She helped me!* I'm really, truly flattered and since she's in such a helping spirit, I going to ask her if she could help us to understand why Edwards Sanders would be allowed to pick up her son from day care." He faced the witness. "Can you help us understand that, Miss Hill? I mean, I don't have a problem with it, personally, but I think it night be fun if everyone knew." He turned back to the jury. "Are you all ready for this?" Then to Deborah. "Why did this man sometimes pick your son up?"

"Because," she cracked acidly, "he the daddy."

Jenners threw his hands up in the air defensively. "There could be no better reason than that...he the Papa. Papa Edward." Jenners motioned for his paper. Deborah thrust it at him meanly. He scanned the sheet. "So that would mean that Papa Edward had to be familiar to the staff at Safety Pins or he wouldn't have been able to just walk away with Junior, now would he?"

"Well, my son wouldn't leave with a stranger anyway."

"Good point. We now know that Warren would only leave the day care with either you or Papa Edward, is that what you would have the Court believe, Miss Hill?"

"That's the truth whether you believe it or not."

"On the sign-out sheet, there is only a space for a single check-in and a single check-out, but it has come to my attention that parents sometimes drop by on their lunch breaks and take their children for a stroll or to get a soda. Usually since the child is coming back and the care-provider is familiar with the adult, there is no official check-out, that is until the end of the day. Five o'clock." Jenners glanced at Deborah. "You do know about this, don't you?"

Deborah hesitated, offering weak laugh. "Why? What's that got to do with anything?"

"Objection!" Elizabeth shouted. "This line of questioning is pointless."

"Overruled."

"You even came by on your lunch break once with Edward and the three of you spent some family time together. About thirty minutes worth. You then brought Warren back. Do you remember that, Miss Hill?"

"Yes, I recall."

"And neither you nor Papa Edward had to sign out Junior, did you?"

"No." The tone was flat; cold.

"Once more now. Is Edward Sanders authorized to pick up your son?"

"Yes, for the hundredth time. Yes."

"So it just could have been that on that day in question, that at lunchtime, Papa Edward could have come by and got Junior. No one would have objected."

"No," Deborah screamed. "That's a lie."

"Objection! He's badgering the witness, Your Honor."

"Overruled.

"Did you ask Edward if he had picked Warren up at lunch that day?"

"I know he didn't."

"How?"

"He would have told me."

"Did he tell he was smoking crack? Did he tell you he was seeing another woman? Did he tell you that he had stolen money out of your purse?"

Deborah said nothing.

"All these things you found out---but after the fact. It just might be possible that Edward Sanders dropped in that day to see his son and spent a few minutes with him as his dope smoking buddies went across the street to buy crack. After all, the police reported that a lot of drug activity goes on there. When his buddies came back, Papa Edward probably told his son to go on back inside, but perhaps Warren didn't go back inside. Perhaps Edward didn't stop to see if his son had actually made it back inside or not."

"Objection! Speculative."

"Your Honor, this is a plausible scenario. I have information that Edward Sanders frequented the crack houses in the neighborhood across from Safety Pins. I have a source, Your Honor, that was frequently with Mr. Sanders. This source says that on many of those instances while he personally went to purchase drugs, Mr. Sanders would drop in and see his son. They even took him for a soda once. All this was unknown to Miss Hill since it was done informally and no record of the departure was noted due to the brief duration of Warren's absence from the premises."

Elizabeth stood up to object, but before she could Judge Williams stared at her sternly. She sat back down.

"So, you see, Miss Hill, maybe Safety Pins was not negligent. Maybe Edward Sanders was."

Jenners sat down.

For better or for worse, it was over. Already he was thinking of California.

12

Jamie Baxter was seven years old. He was having a birthday party and he was enjoying himself immensely. He ran and laughed and played with the other children, eating ice cream and cake. Theresa Baxter smiled happily. Her husband, James, looked on, sullen and glum. Standing next to him was Dr. Hargrove from the Genetics and IVF Institute in Fairfax, Virginia.

"Don't feel bad about it, James. It's only ignorance.....and perhaps a whole lot of fear."

"Fear of what?" James Baxter groaned sadly. "Fear that Jamie's disease is contagious and that by association with him, their kids will be contaminated. Jamie has spinal bifuda, dammit, not mumps, measles or chickenpox. I don't get it, man. And these are educated people. They are supposed to know better."

"To be frank," Dr. Hargrove said, "mainly what it is, is that these people, your neighbors, your peers are highly successful, ambition-driven couples. Look at their life styles. The cars. The money. The vacations. The homes. These are people in search of Utopia, the perfect society and well, when they see your son, it's a reminder that all is not right in the world. Jamie says that sickness and pain and disease do exist and in their self-righteousness, they seek to shelter their children from what they perceive as," he paused, "well, litter on the playground."

"Litter on the playground!" James croaked.

"Yes, to some people, the world is simply one huge, jet-setting playground and to these snobs, individuals like your son are litter on the beach."

"My goodness," Theresa shrieked. "You're serious, aren't you? People truly feel like that, don't they?"

"You can answer that question for yourselves. Just look at all the no-shows among your friends who politely declined the party invitations. It seems mighty convenient that the great majority of them found something else to do all of a sudden."

"None of them found themselves too busy week before last when they were invited over for Theresa's tea."

"That's just it. It's not you or Theresa they're trying to protect their kids from. It's Jamie. The adults will come all day. They're hard and callused, inured to litter, but let Jamie be here and you ask that they bring their children by. No way," Dr. Hargrove reported. "Your son does not reflect or represent the kind of perfection they want their children to see."

"Scumbags," James coughed out angrily. He stared out into the distance, over his manicured lawn. The children played happily, running, jumping shouting merrily. All the other children, other than Jamie, were black. They were having fun, paying no attention to Jamie's "differentness".

Theresa also looked. "But the blacks?"

"They know what discrimination feels like and they easily recognize it in all or any of its manifestations. Too many of them Jamie is just a member of the club. You see all those kids out there?"

Both the Baxters nodded.

"Well, all of them are going to be discriminated against for the rest of their lives. The black ones due to skin color. Jamie, because of his disorder. I have known both of you for quite some time now and I've never detected any racial prejudice and that's great." Dr. Hargrove sighed. "Throughout Jamie's life, he'll have a lot of black friends. They will accept him. A friend is a friend," he shrugged. "There will always be plenty of black boys for friends."

Not if Senator Gaylord had his way, James Baxter thought. He shuddered inside. He kissed his wife. "I must make a trip tomorrow," he whispered in her ear.

He just hoped he wouldn't be too late!

On Thursday, just before 3:00, the trial ground to a halt.

It drew its final breath, expiring softly after Judge Williams performed the legal eulogy, instructing the jury on what the expectations for them were. As a body, they would be required to render a verdict acceptable to the collective conscience. Deliberations would not be easy he warned them and in the next breath scolded them in advance for any major rifts that could possibly arise due to conflicting opinions. It was their duty as citizens to articulate the merits of all they had heard, understood, and felt. And then to let the chips fall where they may.

Up until now, the Judge had said they had been cautioned to hold their own counsel, not to confer among each other or to share opinions, but now the bar of that imposition had been lifted and they were required to bond together and to reach a conclusion healthy to their peace of mind.

Elizabeth sensed intuitively that she had acquitted herself well during closing arguments, but so had Jenners. Both had sought the killing blow. Now there was nothing either could do---except wait. The jury would decide. Deep down Elizabeth was glad it was over. Glancing over at Jenners during the Judge's summation, she could tell he was relieved as well. At last---now---she could see him for the human individual he was.

Irrevocably, the hollowed-out mask of the lawyer fell away and soaked in the aura of exhaustion and battle fatigue, a kindler, more gentler being had emerged. She smiled at him. He smiled back. Both smiles were genuine. And that is how they shook hands. Smiling eyes.

Day One. No verdict.

Day Two. Nothing.

The third day. Still no word from the jury.

That evening when the phone rang, Elizabeth nearly shed her skin. That's how jumpy she was. It was Lou Smith.

"What's up, Lou?"

"Congratulations, counselor. Word has it that you did a real bang-up job in Court. Has everybody buzzing."

"Well, it's not over yet. We both know that anything can fly with a jury."

Lou laughed. "People. So fickle, but no cause for worry. You are going to win by a mile."

"That's nice of you, but I know there has to be another reason for this call."

"Sure bet. Got something I been saving for you. I didn't want to distract you with it during trial, so I held off telling you. I was doing more work on Ronpis, trying to come up with something."

"Nothing?"

"Nothing, but here's the clincher. I got an index card lying on the bed with Ronpis written across it in bold, red letters. My girlfriend, forever the crossword puzzle fanatic, loves to solve things on paper. You know cryptograms, anagrams, logic puzzles, you get my drift?'"

"Yes, but what's the point?"

"As soon as she flopped down on the bed and saw the word Ronpis, she immediately began scrambling the letters and guess what other words the letters R-O-N-P-I-S contain?"

"Tell me. Tell me," Elizabeth squealed. "Tell me."

"Prison. P-R-I-S-O-N."

Elizabeth was silent.

"Miss Sellers. You still there? Miss Sellers."

"I'm here, but I don't get it."

"Neither did I at first until I did some more checking. I decided to look into Jenners' financial history. Recently, his bank account got pumped up real decent. The money was posted recently, but I also found out that in addition to cash, I guess as a gratuity or something, he was given a few shares of stock."

"What AT&T? Sony? Microsoft?"

"Wrong. Stop guessing. You wouldn't come close in a zillion years. The stock is CEA."

"Huh?"

"Yeah, that's right. Ever heard of that outfit?"

"No."

"Figures. C-E-A stands for Correctional Enterprises of America. Correctional, get it. As in prison."

The phone dropped from Elizabeth's hand. Was that it? Was Ronpis the prison/industrial complex? If so, then Ronpis was an even bigger monster than she ever imagined.

She prayed.

Elizabeth could barely drive. She gripped the steering wheel so tightly that her diamond ring cut deeply into her flesh. Her mouth refused moisture and as a result, she had to keep swallowing her own saliva in an attempt to keep her tongue from becoming parched.

She felt almost as if she was rushing to the Alamo or the OK corral, to her untimely death. Yet she never slowed down.

The jury had reached a verdict!

All that had gone before now faded into jaded insignificance and for a lawyer, a jury's verdict was like a final test score. No matter how well you thought you had done, you never actually knew until the grades were passed out. She could feel her heart in her throat. BOOMING! With each breath she took, she could easily imagine her throat expanding and contracting just like a frog's, ballooning out grotesquely, folding in---ballooning out again.

She jetted upstairs.

The Courtroom was already packed, awaiting the judge. A Marshal, upon spying her entrance, swelled with civic pride and went rushing pell-mell to notify Judge Williams. She didn't look at Jenners this time. She just wanted to breathe properly once more.

The VIPs. The Others. They were exchanging notes and pleasantries. They knew this was the end. The last day of class. They shook hands all around. Acquaintances made, soon to be forgotten.

At 1:15, the Judge entered the Courtroom.

The jury followed shortly. They walked in. They took their places, six boxes to the left.

Judge Williams did not honor suspense, would not suspend anxiety. He would be forthright. "Mr. Foreman," he uttered in a stentorian bark, rising high in his chair, "have you and your colleagues concluded your duty and reached a verdict?"

"We have, Your Honor," the black man said, standing, his voice crackling with emotion.

The Marshal, realizing his moment had come, drew himself tall and with three enormous strides stood before the jurors' box, hand outstretched, demanding. Receiving the important document, he retraced his steps---those three giant steps---and handed the Judge the verdict. He instantly began to shrink.

Brooking no delay, the Judge unsheathed the folded paper and bit immediately into the response, not having even the slightest inclination to withhold, for even the tiniest second, the news. He refused to savor the moment for himself, making Elizabeth...Jenners...The VIPs...The Others. All together, collectively----wait.

Instead he said. "The jury finds for the plaintiffs!"

Senator Gaylord flipped through the pages of The Sydney Morning Herald. It was lunchtime. He had a beef appetizer followed by fish followed by a soufflé. He drank a shot of bourbon.

Halfway through the meal, he was approached. A phone call. The Senator refused the house phone and ambled out on the patio where tourists in loud, flower-print shirts gulped blue tequila martinis while half-listening to the live steel band.

Gaylord looked down the bra of a seated, deeply tanned aristocrat while waiting on his phone to get a connection.

He got the connection.

He got the news.

He got mad.

Now, he would get even.

This time while making a second phone call, he discovered another set of boobs to ogle.

"Get me Peters," the Senator growled.

A few seconds later. "Hello, this is Peters."

"Pete, look, this is Gaylord. I'm in Australia at the moment. Do me an immediate favor, will you?"

"Name it."

"Eugene Larry," the Senator snarled, his voice sinister and dark. "Bring the son-of-a-bitch home!"

BOOK II

It had stopped raining.

Elizabeth rolled down the window on her red Audi and felt the lush night rush in scented with honeysuckle sweetness. She swung onto The Plaza, heading towards home, the wet, shiny streets sparkling like a crystal punchbowl. Two lovers strolled across the quiet darkness, enjoying the solitude.

Elizabeth was still shaken.

Riding beside her, Sandra had been quiet for longer than usual. She broke the silence. "Homegirl, why didn't you tell me that Charlotte was all this?"

"I didn't think the Queen City would make much of an impression on you. After all, you're a big city girl from New Jersey. Charlotte," Elizabeth shrugged, "is well, home."

"I love this place," Sandra gushed. "I could stay here always. I'm a big fan."

The Audi raced down The Plaza, the wide avenue laced with trees, their branches hanging low from the weight of the rain. Elizabeth orchestrated the short drive home by executing a complex series of eccentric swings and cut-offs, meaningless right turns and absent stops. *And she still had a follower!* Deliberately, she missed her turn.

"Wasn't that the street where---"

"Yes." Elizabeth spoke softly. "I want to show you some more of Charlotte." She stared into the rearview mirror.

Sandra stared at her watch, faking a yawn. "Girl, this pretty little, hat-box is not going anywhere. Let's call it a night."

"It's only ten," Elizabeth protested, the headlights of the car following her almost on her bumper now. She swung into a Circle K. The car crossed Sugar Creek Road, slowed down, and pulled into a gas station. Stopped. Waited.

"Tell you what,' Sandra offered, "let's buy a gallon of ice cream and go home, snuggle up under the covers and watch a scary movie. Just like in the old days. Get cold and scared, then go to sleep." Sandra laughed, remembering.

Elizabeth laughed back. She was already cold. And scared. The car had its hazard lights on. They pulsed menacingly. Elizabeth shivered.

Sandra, tall, sassy and statuesque got out of the car headed for the entranceway. Elizabeth thought about being left alone. She ran behind Sandra into the store. The car's blinking lights went blank.

Rushing through the door, Elizabeth knew it was not just her imagination. No way. Yet there was no reason to suspect the car was following her. It may not be the same man.

WRONG!

Elizabeth felt eyes on her back. She turned ever so slowly away from the ice cream counter, filled with a greater sense of dread than before. She looked through the store window. She knew.

The car. It was now parked next to her Audi. Hazard lights flashing. DANGER!

The man. Black. Ace-of-Spades black, glared malevolently. DANGER!

"Rum Raisin," Sandra declared happily, clutching the ice cream. "Let's go."

"In a minute," Elizabeth begged. "I need to pick up a few girl things." She slid down the narrow aisle, hovering over the sanitary napkins, peering through a crack she had made on the shelf by moving items out of the way. The car was still parked. The man knew exactly where she was as his eyes were glued to the shelf where they kept the Tampons. She swallowed hard. Fear.

It was the exact same man.

She had noticed him hours ago at The Blumenthal during the final act of the play. He was two rows over, his eyes blazing into her with a rabid, almost morbid fascination. The eyes burned, searing her flesh. He would not look away.

At McCormick's SteakHouse, a few blocks from the theatre, Elizabeth had felt red-hot heat rising from the back of her neck.

It had been him.

With casual nonchalance, he had lifted a toast to her, but instead of sipping the sparkling champagne had instead turned the glass over, upside down, pouring the drink into his food. All the time, he had been grinning. Devilishly.

He then had left.

Ten minutes later, a smiling waiter had humbly approached her table and slipped her a note. Still smiling, the waiter had disappeared. The note, a folded napkin, read: **"I'M YOUR WORST NIGHTMARE!"**

For some reason, she was now beginning to believe it.

"Girl, you coming or what?" Sandra waited at the check-out counter.

Elizabeth hastily gathered a few items and rushed to the front of the store.

The car drove off.

Leaving the parking lot, the man tooted his horn twice as Elizabeth stepped outside. Then farther down the block—twice more. The sound eerily floated back to her ears, a personal message, DANGER!

Relieved that the car was gone, Elizabeth jumped behind the wheel of the Audi and hurriedly made it back onto The Plaza. She drove fast, breathing easier now that the car was nowhere to be seen.

"And I thought I was the one in a hurry," Sandra complained.

"I can't let the ice cream melt, now can I? I know how much you love it hard as a rock."

"Just like I love my men," Sandra giggled.

"Hush now, sista. I don't need you giving me any ideas."

They laughed. Schoolgirls once more.

Elizabeth turned into Hampshire Hills and a chill ripped through her body. The Car! It was there! The horn said BONK! BONK!

On legs barely able to contain her, Elizabeth fumbled for the house keys, hardly noticing the house was dark. Sandra was at her elbow, chatting endlessly. When she pushed the door halfway open, she recoiled from the doorway, bumping into Sandra who pushed her bodily through the door into the darkened living room. Sandra flicked on the light.

"*SURPRISE!*

All over the living room, champagne cords were popped.

"Look, everybody, it's the lawyer of the century," Sandra toasted. "Congratulations, my best friend, on a job well done. We're all so proud of you." Sandra presented Elizabeth to the small gathering. "Hail, the conquering hero."

"You knew," Elizabeth gushed, hugging Sandra. "Girl."

Most of the people in her living room, Elizabeth knew. Everyone from the firm, including the secretaries. A few other lawyers with their companions. One man, however, was a complete stranger. Very VIP'ish. Somebody important.

After about his third drink, the man was towed over by Sandra. "Girlfriend, I'd like for you to meet a good friend of mine, Senator Junius Gaylord." To the Senator. "Senator Gaylord, my best friend in the world, Elizabeth Sellers."

"I couldn't help but hear how you singlehandedly closed all the day care centers in this country," the Senator joked.

"Only a very incompetent one," Elizabeth corrected.

"No need for modesty, you're among lawyers," Gaylord jested."Modesty is virtue lost upon passing the bar exam." He pulled Elizabeth and Sandra to a secluded corner. "I have something for the two of you." Pride beamed in his eyes. He smiled at Elizabeth. "Right now, up on Capitol Hill, you have won many admirers, myself included. For quite some time, a number of my colleagues and myself have been trying to get the day care industry investigated, but we haven't had any success; however now with Safety Pins as a spring board, you have provided us with the needed ammo to get some talks started. So on behalf of all the working mothers in the world, I beg you to accept these tickets to the islands of Hawaii." Gaylord paused dramatically. "Please."

"Thanks," Elizabeth said happily.

"That please me greatly," Gaylord beamed. "Just one other thing," he smiled. "You never got those tickets from me."

They all laughed.

For the time being, the man and his beat-up green Pontiac were forgotten. She was going to Paradise.

As the plane dipped through the clouds, getting low for the landing, Elizabeth gripped Sandra's hand tight in excitement.

"Girl, there's Honolulu."

Out of the window, the geography of the welcoming paradise dramatically held them in rapt attention. It was all sculpted in colorful and spellbinding beauty. The landscape tinted rich and green, the swell of the ocean, blue.

There were cliffs in the background that seemed to sit atop the sparkling sand of the beach and even beyond, almost invisible to the wandering eye, was a dense serene wilderness.   The plane touched down, taxied. Stopped.

"Is this fantasy Island or what?" Elizabeth remarked, "This is so wonderful."

The Hilton Hawaiian Village was located on Waikiki Beach and their room offered a magnificent sweep of the blue water outside. Inside, the hotel boasted a pair of the finest restaurants in Honululu; many shops, nightly entertainment, a waterfalls, a pond, tropical wildlife. Everything.

Leaving the hotel, they visited Waikiki Aquarium where they gawked at sharks and sea turtles. From there, they rounded a meandering curve. More beauty. Tropical green bedecked with oases of white and beige.

Elizabeth let the car window down. A soft, sensual breeze wafted into the car. Another mile or so, the straightway purred into a cat's tail of a curve. They neared Sans Souci Beach close to Diamond Head. They stopped.

Elizabeth jumped. She spotted a Pontiac. Beat up. Green. It was empty. Parked. A tin can monument to her fear. Was he---whoever he was---here? The car was just ahead. Waves of heat glimmered off the chrome bumper, making the car appear as though it was sizzling, a green pot on a white-hot stove.

Decidedly, Elizabeth pushed herself away from her car and strolled quickly in the direction of the Pontiac.

Closer.

And closer.

Still closer.

The car was empty as far as she could tell, and unexpectedly she tried to open the trunk. It was locked.

She moved around to the side, peeking into the backseat. It was empty. She tried the door. It was locked as well.

She raised herself on tip-toes and peered into the front of the car. She saw nothing. Looking behind her to make sure Sandra had gone on to the beach, she depressed the latch on the front door. It clicked. She pulled it open, stepping into the open doorway.

She gasped.

The man!

She attempted to flee, but her weak legs collapsed. She crumpled to the sand.

She shrieked.

In quiet desperation, she clawed frantically at the sand, crawling away. Her face contorted in fear, she stared over her shoulder, scanning the open car door, fully expecting him---the man—to boldly pop out...ax, gun, or knife in hand to finish her off.

Strangely he didn't.

Whimpering sounds gurgled in her throat, trapped there between a scream and a plea for mercy. Yet, nothing. Gripping the back door handle, she pulled herself upright, still ready to run. There was still no movement from inside the car. Maybe the man was asleep. Hurt. Dead.

Silence.

Sun.

That's all there was.

She walked through the sun into the silence, going around the car to the driver's side. She leaned over and peeped. She saw him. Just lying there. Then she noticed that it wasn't him—the man.

She retched. Flecks of dry vomit splayed her lips, dribbling vulgarly onto her chin. Her knees buckled, bending forward and then snapping back, locking in place. Rigid and stiff, she woodenly walked around to the other side of the Pontiac. She had to peek, to look. To see. All fear was gone. Now, all that was important was for her to confirm the recognition, to verify the---whatever it was.

Braced inside the door-well, Elizabeth stooped, sticking her head in. Her stomach bubbled as she fought hard to control the muscles of her bladder and in temporary shock, felt the wetness. Her mouth gaped open, unconcerned with what was happening between her legs. There was no air inside the car. She coughed.

It wasn't grisly. It was almost childish, one of those straw-filled, cotton-stuffed scarecrows on Halloween. It was an effigy, the make-believe version of someone. There were black buttons for eyes. Soft, spongy brillo for hair, grey-tinted. There was a meaty, fleshy nose, and a hollowed-out mouth with smiling upturned lips. So knowable. So...dead!

Inside the car, Elizabeth screamed.

And screamed.

It was an effigy of her father!

She found some identification under the hands. It was her father's driver's license.

Elizabeth yelled this time.

And yelled.

Elizabeth didn't return to the beach that afternoon. It was all she could do not to simply re-pack everything and head home, but since she had spoken with her father, she was somewhat relieved. She had been so glad to hear his voice. She never mentioned his dead likeness.

The next morning with breakfast out of the way, Elizabeth and Sandra paid respects to the dead at the National Memorial Cemetery of the Pacific. This ancient volcanic crater was the most visited site on the island. It was called PUOWAINA meaning 'Hill of human sacrifice'. Over five million people made the trek yearly.

They also paid a visit to Pearl Harbor to view the USS Arizona Memorial which was built over one of the battleships sunk during World War II.

"Let's get to moving," Sandra declared, "that's enough death for me. Let's go cloud-walking."

On the island, there is only one place to go cloud-walking and that is on the mountain of Maui where hikers traverse belts of dense fog and rain forests, marching past farms and ranches. The upcountry.

Sandra and Elizabeth arrived similarly attired in hiking shorts and heavy boots, their faces, arms and legs lightly smeared with a mixture of sunscreen and an aromatic insect repellent. They were ready to climb. At least Sandra was. Elizabeth just didn't want to be alone.

She had lain awake most of the night, trying to piece together the puzzle, but she could conclude nothing, except that she was afraid. At the thought of fear, a nervous surge of adrenaline shot through her tense body, tingling her senses. Every muscle was on stand-by. Fight. Or flight.

Now, of a sudden, this hike did not seem like such a good idea. If someone was trying to kill her---she didn't know why. Or even if someone was simply trying to scare her---still she didn't know why. All she knew clearly was that if either of those alternatives were, at any time, to be pursued, there would be no better moment than now. The depressing gloom of the mountains offered a perfect backdrop for murder.

Elizabeth glanced warily over her shoulder at the others in the hiking group. She recognized no one. None of the six seemed suspicious so she glanced over Sandra's shoulder, searching in the mist for him. The man who Ace-of-Spades black.

A short, squat man, perhaps thirty five was the tour guide. He was bronzed from the sun, in need of a shave, and dressed less-severely than the rest of them. When he spoke, he sounded like Don Ho, the words gushing out of his full moon face, slowly melodic.

"Welcome fellow travelers," he intoned, "I hope you are all ready for adventure. Before we leave, please make sure your canteens are filled." He smiled. "Drink plenty of water. We'll start in only moments and it will take us, depending on speed, about five hours to complete the trail roundtrip. It is listed as difficult and challenging, but I promise you it will be fun and easy." His wandering eyes fell upon Elizabeth. "I have never lost a traveler yet on one of these expeditions."

Elizabeth looked over Sandra's shoulders again.

The trail ascended slightly at first, nothing more than an elevated rise where they stopped to be patiently lectured about the rare snails. Rare or not, they were still ugly, Elizabeth thought and no more precious. She refused to personally examine one as it was passed from hand to hand, caressed as if it was a house pet. Uggh.

Rounding out of the snail plantation, they found themselves in a deep bog of violets and silversword plants. As Elizabeth could have guessed, they were also rare. She almost laughed, knowing that nature is usually so ample when it comes to plants and animals left alone without the destructive hand of man attendant upon them.

Suddenly, they were in the aeries, cloud-walking. Once more, Elizabeth felt unsafe. She huddled closer to Sandra whom she nudged closer to the center of the group.

Mist fell coldly upon her slender shoulders as the thick, dense clouds carved long, dark swatches of blackness where the sunlight couldn't shoo away the dark. She wanted to see. Darkness was haute couture for evil, an evening gown for mischief. Cover for the Ace-of-Spades man.

Daylight.

Then just as suddenly, darkness again.

Elizabeth sighed, relieved. This was eerie. Now, no one spoke. It was as though her fear was contagious and that she had infected everyone. To reduce their vulnerability, everyone moved closer to each other, sardine-like tight, and looked out in the darkness, wanting to be sure that nothing lurked in the neat, dark patches that had deserted the light of day.

The collective fear was real.

Silence.

Etched at the fringe of the next looming cloud, more foggy blackness loomed, a half-opened door to terror, but they trooped in just the same, flashlight-bearing warriors groping for security.

Something---not them—moved in the non-light. Everyone froze. The darkness was occupied.

"What was that thump?" Sandra asked. "Who's drumming?"

"That was only---"

BOOMABOOMABOOM!

The drum sound beat closer, thumping in the shadows. Right there beside them.

"You see, we are in the upcountry---keep moving everyone---and it is not usual for the cowboys to--

"I don't care if it's cowboys, Indians, or the lil' drummer boy. I want to be able to see them," an elderly man said.

BOOM!

Daylight again.

The tour guide laughed mischievously. "I am sorry," he apologized. He stepped back into the depths of lingering night and returned with a recorder. He touched a remote button.

BOOMABOOMABOOM!

"A little something extra." He smiled. "Nothing shakes up the morning like a hint of danger." He replaced the drum machine back into the shadow of darkness.

"No more of that shit," the elderly man snarled. "You're a fucking tour guide, not Alfred Hitchcox, so can we get on with this hike?"

"C'mon, everybody, it was just a gag," Sandra giggled. "Don't throw the poor man over a cliff."

A pale glint of sunlight slivered between the clouds and a rainbow appeared in the far distance.

"Look," Sandra cried in delight, "a rainbow. Take us up so we can stand under it."

"Yeah," someone else chimed, "that would be much better than standing here."

The course became more grueling along the ridgeline, becoming almost vertical. Talk became scarce and the sounds most heard were grunts and groans as the hikers labored to keep up.

It was time to eat by the time they reached Waikomoi Preserve, a high elevation rain forest that was the habitat of eight of the birds on Hawaii's endangered species list. The tour guide proudly pointed out all eight, and then allowed them to eat lunch.

"Rest well," he cautioned, "for next we climb to the 7 Sacred Pools at Kipahulu."

Elizabeth's food wouldn't go down. Still, she nibbled away trying not to reveal her recurring nervousness, but it was back gnawing at her. She possessed the terribly real sense of undeniable doom. It hung over her head, looming, impending, ready to spill unspeakable torture upon her.

For sure, the Ace-of-Spades man was not far away.

Then suddenly, the tour guide was on his feet. "To the 7 Sacred Pools," he commanded.

Upward, the path led. It snaked and twisted, tripping through trees heavily scented with the aroma of fermenting guavas. The trees, the farther they travelled up the incline, became more knitted, narrowing, and in some places, obscuring the path until there was nothing but wild grass. It was like entering a forest tunnel. The darkness grew, maturing from nature's green to almost black. Once they cleared the trees, they sat atop a color-splashed promontory. They hovered so closely to a man-made geyser that icy cold water sprinkled down on them, making the landing wet and slippery.

"Behold!" the tour guide announced, pointing across the divide.

The promontory was breathless. The sun burst through, giving life to shadows, misty-covered apparitions that slithered across the mountains.

Elizabeth felt death. She grabbed Sandra's hand, pulling her back.

"What's the matter, girlfriend?" Sandra smiled.

"I-I don't feel good about this."

"It's just the altitude, Miss Lizzy. Everything's okay. Trust me."

When they had reached the rail, Elizabeth was delirious with fear. Every inch of her body was drenched in it. Instinctively, she moved closer to Sandra, but sensing movement behind her, she dazedly spun around. It was the elderly gentlemen, taking pictures. She let out a sigh of gratitude.

As she moved to turn away, the geyser erupted, sprouting water. For a brief second, everyone covered up, protecting themselves from the quarter-sized goblets of water. Sandra snapped her photo. The elderly man did also. Elizabeth started to protest, but the geyser came alive again, sprouting mist, sprouting water. This time Elizabeth automatically ducked and spun around. The fear was gone. She hugged herself, crouching low, giggling, but when she looked around----Sandra was gone also.

Everyone was looking down...down...down...

She looked also.

There was Sandra, falling, swooping low over the cliff, tumbling down...down...down. Death.

Sandra had forgotten to scream.

Elizabeth didn't.

Elizabeth lost consciousness. When she was revived, she found herself in what at first appeared to be a church. It wasn't. It was simply a clapboard rest area. Her first impulse was to ask for Sandra, but she knew. She had seen herself how her best friend had died, tumbling and bouncing off hard, jagged rocks as if she had been a plastic mannequin. How horrible it had been.

A medic stood over her, smiling, reassuring her that she would be just fine. He started to mention something about the other American black woman, but decided against it as if any reminders of the accident might be enough to cause her to lose consciousness again.

Someone brought her a phone. "You may wish to notify someone about the unfortunate......"

They left the phone. They left also.

Elizabeth dialed her parents' home in Charlotte. The phone rang. Nothing. She then called the office. After two rings, she was babbling into the phone hysterically.

"Calm down, Elizabeth, please," the secretary pleaded. "We've been trying to contact you all morning. Did you get any of our messages?"

"Messages? No," Elizabeth sobbed. "I'm not at the hotel. Oh, Cynthia, there has been a terrible accident----
"

"You know?" Cynthia was surprised.

"Know?" Elizabeth asked, puzzled. "Know what?"

"About the accident?"

"Of course, I was there."

"There? Where? With whom?' Now Cynthia was puzzled.

"Sandra."

"No, I don't mean Sandra."

Fear caught in Elizabeth's throat. "If you don't mean Sandra, just who do you mean?"

"I'm sorry," Cynthia said, "but you had better come home right away."

"Why? What's wrong?"

"It's your father, Elizabeth. He's dead."

Elizabeth choked back tears. Disbelief.

"He was killed in a car accident."

Before she lost consciousness, Elizabeth remembered thinking that something very strange was going on and one word came to mind. RONPIS.

After the funeral, Elizabeth tried to throw herself back into her work. Anything to escape the suffering and the grief. She went to work three days in a row before she accepted the fact that the ruse wasn't working. She needed a moment to heal. She would take a leave of absence.

Just before leaving the office, she stared at the small pile of unanswered memos and unreturned phone calls. There was one number in particular that had kept showing up. A number she didn't recognize and there was no name, personal or professional, attached. She dumped everything in the trash.

At the office door, she stopped. Turned. And went back to the trash receptacle. She stared at the number suspiciously. Dialed.

"Hello." A man's voice. White. Not so young.

"This is Elizabeth Sellers of Truman, Daniels, Thornton, and Bailey."

"At last," the voice breathed, "I've gotten in touch with you."

"It does appear that way, Mr......"

"My name is not important, but I'm a friend."

"Is there anything else, sir? I'm very busy. Please be brief."

"Eugene Larry," the voice said distinctly. "Remember that name."

James Baxter hung up the phone. He couldn't have been any briefer than that.

On Saturday, Elizabeth met Lou in Marshall Park and begged him to take control of the Ronpis investigation full-time.

"Personally, I'm intrigued." Lou sipped his pineapple juice, bit into his garden burger.

"So you think there might be a conspiracy?"

Lou laughed grimly. "There are conspiracies," he mused, "and there are conspiracies. But, I must be honest, I have always felt there was a conspiracy against black men in this country. As a black man myself, I can feel it in the air. And it's been around for a while."

"Maybe," Elizabeth offered, "this is the latest installment."

"You make it seem like a lay-away plan."

"Why not?" Elizabeth countered. "If America is so deathly afraid of young, black males, why not simply nip the problem in the bud? Kill them off while they are still babies, long before they have a chance to cause white America problems."

Lou thought about that. This was America where the natural obsession was the fear of the black man. He thought about the Tuskegee experiment, drugs in the black community, AIDS, black neighborhoods being built on toxic dump sites. No, the notion was not too far-fetched.

"You know," he grimaced, "there just might be something to your September 1st conspiracy, but where is the common thread?"

"The date. That's the link."

"Okay, say it is, but what is it a link to? We've got five black males known to be born on September 1st. Four are toddlers, all almost killed at the same place, a day care center named Safety Pins. All four of these shorties were recruited by Ronpis which, by the way, doesn't exist. The fifth brother, Eugene Larry, although he was born on September 1st doesn't fit the mold." Lou drummed his pen on the notepad. "But, thanks to my girlfriend, it is easy to believe that Ronpis is a code name for Correctional Enterprises of America, and Eugene Larry has spent time, a lot of it, in prison----"

Elizabeth prodded him on. "Keep going. Keep going."

"This is where the train runs out of tracks."

"But what about the murders of my father and my best friend?"

"Hell, yeah, there's something there. What?"

"You haven't forgotten about the dark-skinned man in the green car, have you?" Elizabeth face tightened. "I'm not giving up, so forget that possibility." She looked at Lou. "I need you, brotha."

"I'm in" Lou said. "Let's make it do what it do."

Deborah Hill awoke quickly and rolled away from the light. She made it just in time. The blade of the knife plunged softly into her pillow. She screamed, shrieking wildly. She yanked the long knife from the hand of her son, Warren.

Instead of beating him, she clutched him, dragging him to her bosom. She cried and cried and cried. What was wrong with her baby?

No one seemed to know. Not even the doctors at John Hopkins. Last month, she had flown up to Baltimore, taking Warren with her. The doctors had scheduled him for a battery of neurological tests after doctors in Charlotte had determined that his problem was not a result of his being hit by a car. They decided it was rooted in a rare neuro-developmental disorder that turned happy youngsters into sullen, irritable monsters.

Dr. Donovan Aaron had performed three days of testing on Warren. On the first day, he had welcomed Deborah into his office, filling her with the promise of both a diagnosis and a cure. He had playfully chatted with Warren as he explained to Deborah that there was no need for alarm as Warren probably suffered from a rare, uncommon disorder that occurred in fewer than ten out of a hundred children on a yearly basis. He patted Deborah's hand paternally as he had her undress her son for the initial physical examination.

Returning the next day, Dr. Aaron, still confident and smiling, patiently explained to Deborah that the physical exam had turned up nothing remarkable about Warren, meaning that his overall physical demeanor was healthy. He also conveyed, with somewhat less enthusiasm, that the hematology report on her son had uncovered no blood abnormalities.

After their talk, the doctor dismissed Deborah to the outer office. He said Warren needed to be checked for viral infection. He also decided to perform a bone marrow test. "Be back in a jiffy," he smiled.

The next morning, Dr. Aaron was no longer smiling. He was stiff and business-like. "Today," he announced, "I will conduct a brain scan."

By that afternoon, the neurological tests were complete and it was clear to Deborah that Dr. Aaron had no idea what was wrong with her son. Sputtering about, he fussed over a chart, then presented it to

Deborah. To her, it looked like a photograph of noodle soup.

"I'm sorry," Dr. Aaron finally confessed, "but I can't find anything wrong with your son. I simply do not know how to explain his behavior. I apologize."

Two days after returning home, Warren killed the cat.

Any time she questioned him as to why he did certain things, his response was always the same.

"Warren, why did you strangle the cat?"

"The TV told me to do it, Mama."

"Warren, why did you hit the little girl with a stick?"

"The TV told me to do it, Mama."

"Warren, why did you set the bathroom on fire?"

"The TV told me to do it, Mama."

And he would turn back to watching television.

Deborah didn't know what to do. If she refused to let him watch TV, he would cry incessantly. Anyway, she knew it wasn't the television that had made him do any of the horrible things he did. After all, the only thing he wanted to watch were those tapes the friendly man on her job had given her. Even though Warren seemed addicted to them, what harm could they do? They were approved for children and introduced by a children's educational watchdog group. As always, she wondered how much damage could puffy, doughy cartoon characters with names like Mr. Happy and Miss Shy do.

TV, she concluded, was the least of her problems.

It really didn't occur to him until later that night just what it was that he had accomplished, but when the sleepy realization fully dawned upon him, he couldn't rest.

Jack Torrence felt powerful.

SuperMan!

Once the notion of his budding superiority began to set in, he was obsessed. Power was a tangible force. He dashed to the full-length mirror in the bathroom and literally ripped the shirt from his torso, half-expecting to see bulging muscles. He had never experienced anything quite like this before and nothing had ever felt as good.

He stared at himself in the mirror, ogling his pale, puny frame. No muscles, but no matter. The power was there nonetheless. He threw back his head, cupped his hands around his mouth and yelled like Tarzan. Loud. Primitive.

His wife came barging through the hallway. "What the hell is going on?" she asked sleepily.

He kissed her cheek. "Go back to bed. You wouldn't understand." He yelled again, beating his chest. Over the years, he had learned that superior men never masked their emotions when their moment of truth arrived. Some cried. Some prayed. Some got drunk. He yelled like Tarzan.

A few weeks ago, he had found out about InnerTalk, subliminal software which flashes positive affirmations to computer software users as they use their terminals. The FCC which had banned the use of subliminals in broadcasting in the 70s had given their tacit approval for their return and since last November, both government and corporate agencies had been snapping up the programs.

The programs offered over 9,000 affirmations from bowling to spirituality, but none of these had interested him. What had caught his eye was software for hyperactive children that flashed messages such as "*I can be still*" or "*Concentration is natural and easy.*"

It had hit him like a ton of bricks!

What if?

Once he had discovered that a firm called Motivision sold a $250 box that plugged into the television so that you could get flashed while watching any regular TV show, he knew he had a plan. A little gift for his puppet, Warren. If, he had reasoned, flashing could make a kid sit still, it could also make him kill!

The rest was simple technology. Any jack-leg electronic whiz-kid could do it. He had bought a whole slew of those new, goofy, blob-like educational cartoons and had doctored them with negative subliminals. "*I hate Mommy. Kill the cat. Burn the house down.*"

The hardest part had been getting the damned videos to Deborah Hill, but where there's a goody-two-shoes, that is the way.

Torrence kicked off his pajama bottoms and strode purposefully in the bedroom. He snatched the covers from his wife's body and threw himself down upon her.

"Me Tarzan. You Jane"

Then he made her scream like never before.

William Sloan was the most popular kid at Tiger Lily Day Care Center! He wallowed in the admiration of all the other children. He was a highly recognized day care celebrity. The little girls swooned as he passed, dying for him to notice them. The young boys were constantly fighting to walk beside him and to be admitted to his inner circle. It was a well-known fact among all the children that you had to have something going for yourself in order to merit the company of Lil' William. The Boy-King didn't squander his largesse.

Tamara Sloan didn't understand it at all. Ever since Safety Pins had closed and she had transferred her son to Tiger Lily, he had become an overnight sensation. She was amused and pleased. He even got phone calls. Pretty, little girls just checking up on him to make sure he had made it home safely. A lady's man and not yet four.

Still, she didn't understand.

Alfred McManus did. He understood clearly. And with this knowing came a heady intoxication, an euphoric giddiness that was both fresh and exhilarating. Sometimes when he thought about it, it filled him with pride so swollen in his chest that he felt it would rent him asunder. He told himself that he would have to employ greater self-restraint or else he would do nothing all day but congratulate himself.

He high-fived himself.

At William Sloan's age, most pre-school kids were just learning to run and to jump easily, to copy the actions and words of adults. They could draw squares, circles and could work simple puzzles. They enjoyed books, board games, drums, and bells. They desired to be fascinated.

And William Sloan fit the bill. He was fascinating. *More importantly, he had candy!* Instant celebrity. Every day, once his mother had dropped him off at day care, William would casually ask to go to the restroom. Once there, he would lock himself inside one of the stalls and wait. As always, when the coast was clear, the janitor would saunter in and pretend to clean the mirrors. He would always knock on the bathroom stall three times to let William know they were alone. Then young William would report everything he had heard or seen anyone do.

"My Mama was kissing a man in bed last night. Little Bobby peed in his pants yesterday. My uncle said

that the white man is the devil. They say the man at the store sells stale cookies."

When William was finished, the man would slide him some candy samples under the stall. He would then whisper that the rest of the candy was in William's locker and that they would meet again in the morning.

McManus was nurturing a spy or if you preferred the more localized rendering, he was turning William into a rat, a snitch. With the War on Drugs in full swing, McManus saw enormous potential in developing a tightly-controlled organization of tattle-tales, professional snitchers that he would rent out to the feds as well as to local and state law enforcement agencies. Not only would his professional rats be available to crack drug case, they would be on loan for any crime from domestic violence to armed robbery. He would deploy them across the country. *Rent-A-Snitch.* When you needed one, a rat would be available---for a price, of course.

McManus didn't doubt the success of his future enterprise. With law enforcement agencies across the country strapped for manpower, his rental scheme would blossom nicely. Would become as huge as Avis or Hertz car rentals. He would have a staff of about a dozen snitchers working full-time on various cases at all times. As soon as a big crime happened, he would be ready to dispense his workers to see what they could come up with. He then would be in position to sell juicy gossip to the tabloids all the while rotating his puppets in and out of prison. That would keep the Senator off his back.

McManus was delirious with dollar signs, but first he knew he had to develop the Sloan kid. He foresaw no problems. None whatever. The boy adored the limelight and he knew that as long as he had access to candy, he would remain top dog. He also knew what he had to do to keep the candy coming----tell everything he knew!

By George, McManus quaked, he was going to make his way into Forbes Magazine. That's how filthy rich he was going to become.

Rent-A-Snitch.

Who woulda thought?

James Baxter's hands were shaking. He tried to write. Couldn't. Anyway, if he could write, what words would he use? How did or would he inform the Senator that it was his full intention to withdraw from the project? He would be branded a coward and treated as a traitor, but would they let him live? That was the major question. Would the Senator have him killed?

Baxter knew the answer. He realized that if he mailed such a resignation to the Senator, he knew what the bold-lettered response would read. It would say: **"PLEASE BE ADVISED THAT APPROPRIATE MEASURES WILL BE TAKEN PROMPTLY!"** It would be signed simply: Junius.

Without delay, Baxter thought better of the impending resignation to Senator Gaylord. He would have to invent a more creative way to wiggle out of his dreaded obligation. It would be simply impossible for him to manipulate the life of another human being. Life, he had come to realize, should be lived on its own terms and not corralled into a maze for either fun or profit. Thank God, he had recognized that before it had become too late. He would not discriminate against another person, no matter how weak, defenseless or unknowing. He wouldn't do it for Jamie's sake.

Still he had to face the Senator. That evening he did.

"Would you care for something to drink? A rum punch, perhaps." The Senator was gracious.

"Don't mind if I do," Baxter returned, trying to sound casual. "A martini with an olive, please."

Handing Baxter the drink, Gaylord sat opposite him. "You're never going to get a promotion at the rate you're going. All the others are making you eat their dust." There was a twinkle of merriment in his eyes. "What's your strategy? What wonderful schemes are you hatching in that brilliant mind of yours? Something stupendous, I would hope." Senator Gaylord set aside his glass. He was expecting a response.

Baxter awkwardly attempted to duplicate the Senator's air of nonchalance. He sat his drink down and leaned back in the chair. "I never realized promotions came along with the job." He smiled. "Just imagine that in a decade or two I could be President of Puppets International."

"Hard work and dedication are the formula for success," the Senator joked. "The sky is the limit, provided you ever get off the ground."

Baxter felt intimidated by the calm, poised demeanor of Senator Gaylord. He squirmed a bit. He knew that his nervousness was detected and that his fear would be sniffed out eventually, but it didn't matter. Much. He would stall for time until he was definite about his course of action. Right now, it was too damned early to burn bridges and under no circumstances could he tip his hand. That would be foolish. Stupid. Deadly. What have I gotten myself into, Baxter wondered.

"Look, Senator,' Baxter whined, "I admit I'm off to a slow start, but nothing I've planned has seemed suited to what I really want to do, so I've just been trying to find my medium. I, well, actually, it's my intention to do something with my approach that is radically novel, very different from the direction any of the others have taken." Baxter leaned forward in his chair. "I have really been studying the case history of Eugene Larry and it is my desire to modify my approach to fit your model. As you know, when you began your work---"

"I hope you don't intend to lecture me about my past achievements." Senator Gaylord spoke annoyingly. "I simply need to be made to understand your great reluctance to throw yourself into your job. In comparison with the others, you have done nothing. I need you to explain that too me and believe me," the Senator snarled, "I'm beginning to feel as if you have eroded the breadth of your obligation too me and I don't want to hear any more of that bullshit about you following in my footsteps."

The office seemed to get chillier as the Senator got up to freshen their drinks. Baxter spoke to Gaylord's back, glad to avoid the probing scrutiny of his eyes. "I can recognize your concern, but---"

Without turning, the Senator spoke over his shoulder, interrupting. "Fuck my concern. What are you going to do to alleviate it? That is what I want to hear. All I've heard so far is evaporated piss." He spun around, walked across the office, faced Baxter. "You do recall that I did inform each of you that once we cast our lots together that there would be no turning back and that I wouldn't tolerate any laxity whatsoever. You recall that, don't you, Mr. Baxter?"

"Yes." Baxter gulped hard, swallowing his fear-tainted saliva. "I recall that."

"Dammit, Baxter, am I going to have a problem with you?" He unloosened his tie, shaking loose the knot. "I don't have time to sit around and pussyfoot with you. Too much is at stake here. You do understand that, don't you?"

Baxter feared Gaylord was close to striking him. He shrank away, pushing himself deeper into the arms of the chair. He thought he saw the Senator nod slightly to himself in acknowledgment of the cowardice he exhibited by moving away.

"You're a pussy, aren't you?" he spat accusingly. He swiftly reached between Baxter's legs, digging into his groin. "Where's your fucking balls, you bastard?"

Baxter yelped, pushing the hand away.

"I'll be damned," Gaylord snorted, walking back to where he had left his drink. "I'll be damned," he muttered again. "Who'd have figured you'd go soft." He sipped from his drink. "Are you really that much of a pussy?"

The retort stung, hanging in the air. It resided there, lingering.

"No," Baxter finally whispered.

"Good." Gaylord set down his drink. He walked across the office and extended his hand. "We both are going to forget this little exchange ever took place. No one will ever know." Then with a sinister tone, whispered. "It still may not be too late for you to salvage your respect with me, but you have got to hump it." He withdrew his hand. "Now, get the fuck out of my office."

For the next three days, James Baxter stayed locked away in the guest room at his home, praying and fasting. Each day he grew angrier. He was no pussy. The Senator would soon find that out.

On the fourth day as he had promised his wife, he emerged. After he had showered, his wife prepared a hot meal for him and even though he had not eaten, he still did not have much of an appetite. As he toyed with his food, his wife look worried, begging him to tell her what was wrong. He started clumsily, then fell into a thick silence, stuffing cabbage and green peas into his mouth.

Later as she cleared the table, he held her hand tightly. "I'm sorry, sweetheart. I'm not ready to talk yet."

"But it's killing you, whatever it is. You can't keep it in or it will destroy you. If you can't talk to me, tell someone. If it's a secret that horrible, go to confession." A tear came to her eyes. "You cannot continue to carry this great burden by yourself. Can't you see that it's crushing you?"

Misty-eyed, Baxter looked at his wife sadly. "Bring me the phone."

"Please, honey, call someone...talk."

He made a call. Almost hung up. Then.

"Hello."

"Hello, Miss Sellers, I hate to disturb you at home, but I need to talk with you."

"To whom am I speaking?" Elizabeth politely inquired.

Before he could answer, his own phone pulsed. An incoming call. "Hold on for a second, Miss Sellers. I have a call. I'll only be a second."

Baxter clicked over.

"Baxter," Senator Gaylord intoned. "I've been worried about you." His voice was dark, morose. "I understand that you haven't been to work all week and I was rather concerned. Are you doing okay?"

"Yes, Senator, I'm fine. Thank you."

"Good. Very well, then." Gaylord paused. "Baxter?"

"Yes, Senator."

"I'm depending on you."

"Yes, Senator. I know."

"Then don't let me down.'

Baxter ended the call and pressed his head between his hands.

"You had someone on the other line," his wife excitedly reminded him.

"It's no use," Baxter groaned. "I'm in too deep for help."

Baxter trudged off to get a drink, leaving the telephone number on the kitchen table. His wife glanced at the name, Elizabeth Sellers, and then stuffed the number in her bra.

I glided in on the wings of night, smelling of beer, imitating death. I was bathed in menace. I basked in it. Fear had become my essence and as I inhaled the pale stink of it, I glowed. I was cemetery cool. Crazed. No longer what I was. No longer caring. The ball-squeezer had changed me.

I saw her. Felt hatred. Remorse alien to my senses. I could have killed her, would have killed her. Would have enjoyed the lust of it, but she was to be spared. Damn!

When she arose, the dawn infant pink upon the morning, I was there. Close. As she climbed out of bed, pulling herself from the repose of sleep, it was my eyes that saw her first, drinking in every detail of her feminine essence, but seeing her naked aroused nothing. I was coiled-springed death on a leash. I was permitted only to despoil her with my eyes, my presence, my menace instead of being set loose upon her like a black, dark demon. To kill. To destroy. To end.

Throughout the day I had breathed heat upon her, constricting her chest tight with pain. I visited fear upon her, but when she had looked over her shoulder to see, I had moved beyond her vision. She only knew that I had been there. Somewhere.

If only I could kill her.

That would release me. Let me climax.

It had been like this for days now. Playing with her. Toying with her, wading in the shallow waters of her terror-filled existence when now I longed to take the plunge. To rip her heart out.

I was as much a victim as she was. I was caged, pulled taut, unresolved. My mind felt tortured. It was almost like listening to a piano concerto, your favorite piece being masterfully delivered, soaking you in rapture. You float on every chord, having sex with every note until the piece swirls and swoons, heightening to its royal finale, when the pianist, knowing full well the pain he will subject you to, gets up and walks away, leaving the last, final note unplayed.

Oh, what unresolved agony.

The mind screams. Hollers. Begs. That last note must be played. It must! That was how I felt. This bitch was the final note.

Aaahhhghh!

<<<<<

Elizabeth rose shakily from her knees and steadied herself. Nothing or no one was hiding under her bed. Now, she had to check the closet. This is how it had been for her, checking and rechecking, searching. For the last week or so, she had the distinct impression that she was no longer alone. Not even at her new home.

She gingerly opened the utility closet. Empty. Slowly, she pulled it closed. She froze. A light ran our from under the door to the guest room. With caution, she drew near and standing at the doorway, looked over her shoulder wondering. Was she alone? She clasped the doorknob, but resisted the urge to turn it, to twist it open, to stare inside the confines of the comfortable room. It would be vacant, wouldn't it? She slid close to the door, pressing her ear against the wood, listening. She strained to hear. Anything. She heard nothing, only silence. It meant nothing because it was silence without conviction, silence without the promise of emptiness and that is what she prayed for---silence mated with emptiness.

She listened harder, her right ear resting flush upon the wood-grain, trying to ferret out any discernible aural clue that the room was bare of human presence. At last, her brain gave consent. Reluctantly, she pressed her sweaty hand onto the doorknob, squeezing and twisting. Opening.

Abruptly.....

BONK! A car horn!

Elizabeth's knees grew into jelly. She twisted her head violently, flinging it towards the sound. It came again.

BONK!

She knew it would. She barged through the house, bumping into an armchair. She bounced off, not slowing down, scooting around an end table, running fast. She snatched the front door open. She glinted into the darkness. The green Pontiac was there, pulsing menace, hazard lights thumping.

BONK! BONK!

Elizabeth fumbled inside her pocket and ran to her car. The Pontiac was moving slow, daring her. The Audi roared to life. The hazard lights on the other car blinked once more, then off. The Audi pulled into the street. The other car, the green Pontiac zoomed away.

The Audi gave pursuit.

They headed south, blazing down I-77, darting in and out of traffic, passing the moon as it sparkled over Woodlawn Road. The Pontiac waited until the last second before swinging off onto the exit, rounding the curve and charging back into the traffic, moving west. Elizabeth was not far behind, losing only a few seconds negotiating the hairpin turn. Bojangles. McDonalds. Krispy Kreme. The Holiday Inn. They all meshed into a single blur as she bumped across the railroad tracks as Nation's Crossing.

North. Every time she attempted to draw close in the red Audi, she found that the Pontiac had more to give. She stomped down hard on the gas pedal as the Pontiac's brake lights flared angrily like two red nostrils as the Remount Road exit seemed to beckon.

Elizabeth's hands tightened on the wheel. The Pontiac went for it. The Audi was in close pursuit, nearing the turn, full speed. A patch of grass abutted the exit and Elizabeth slammed on her brakes, forcing the Audi to loop recklessly out of the tight turn onto the grass and back into the northbound lane. The Pontiac had done the same. *She was on his ass!*

Elizabeth's heart pounded. She was sweaty. Drenched. She stabbed her finger on the console. The driver's side window eased partially down as a stream of fleeting air rushed in, mingling with the heat of her body. She looked away. A thick cloud of white, puffy smoke shot out of the Pontiac's tailpipe, billowing up, turning invisible. Her body sent signals. Slow down. Cease. Desist. All commands were ignored, dismissed. She was in the strange grip of a powerful sweltering inner heat that tossed her towards one of two options.

Suicide.

Or homicide.

Both cars sped on. This time the Pontiac did fly onto an exit. Elizabeth didn't flinch, didn't observe which exit it was. She didn't give a damn. Nothing was substantial, but the anger, the night. The green Pontiac.

She was more animated now. Ambitious. Determined to force a battle. They turned again, red light flashing. Through it, they both flew. Not slowing down. Elizabeth was enveloped in cold sweat. She didn't let the window up. Instead, she focused intently on the constant motion of the car ahead, expecting lateral movement to the left or right at any moment. When it came, she would be ready.

Another hairpin turn and they were barreling down an empty street alongside a railroad trestle. Familiar. Very familiar. Too familiar.

"Damn!" she cursed aloud before stopping. He had led her back home.

BONK! BONK!

The green Pontiac did magic. It disappeared into the night.

BONK! BONK

On Thursday morning, Elizabeth awoke at 2:30 am. She realized that she hadn't slept well and was trying to rehearse a mantra to help her return to sleep when she noticed the blue light blazing from the television. She raised herself weakly on her elbow, staring blankly. She remembered cutting it off. From the living room, there was a steady stream of chatter. The television. At once her attention was drawn to the kitchen. Music. *Waylon Jennings was on her radio!*

She leaned over the side of the bed and fished out her bedroom slippers. She stuffed her feet into them and hastily fastened her robe around her. She reached under the pillow for the gun. It was gone! In its place was a pack of unopened cigarettes. Newports. The brand her father had smoked.

She tried to stifle her rising fear by speaking to herself. She hurried to the kitchen, grabbing a knife. On the way out, she clicked the radio off. The country twang died. She raised her arm shoulder level high, knife poised, extended, ready to strike.

The house was quiet now, dark. The television blank. She felt ill at ease. She reached for the remote control, studied it, punching the button. OFF. She tossed the remote on the bed, turned her back, jumped. Scared. The TV was back on. With sound. Then the one in the den blasted on, filling the house with noise.

After a brief second or two. Intense quiet.

Both TVs went OFF.

The eerie silence was aggravated by the hard ragged sound of her thumping heart and jagged breathing. She half-turned, twisting her torso this way and that, staring glassy-eyed at the TVs.

They had popped back ON.

Noiseless.

Elizabeth crumpled to a heap on the floor, rolled up in a ball, sobbing uncontrollably.

"Bastard," she yelled in a dull, uninspired voice. "Bastard."

It was late Thursday afternoon when Elizabeth picked herself up from the floor. She felt disheveled, particularly out-of-sorts. She did not understand how she had arrived at this point in her life. The thing she had sought most—victory—had now exposed her to so much grief, but it was still her battle. She would not surrender. She prayed that her adversary---The Ace-of-Spades –Man would be ready to engage her in physical combat soon. Or else she would be defenseless. Her fragile mental facilities were in jeopardy and she weakly acknowledged that she could snap at any moment.

She felt oppressed mentally, but there was no self-pity. Only a patient resolve to see the moment through. She dragged herself through the ritual of a shower, feeling eyes upon her nakedness, violating the sanctity of scrubbing herself clean. She drew in a breath. Let him look, whoever he was; wherever he was. He couldn't have her. She would die first, but instantly the still voice within reassured her that sex was not the issue. Maybe mental rape, the possible ravage of her soul. Nothing physical. Elizabeth was not even sure he wanted her dead. Just diminished.

An ocean-deep sense of paranoia wrapped itself around her and she wished for death. Well, a part of her did. The other part, the sane part, was powered by the motivation of revenge.

Her psychic wounds bled.

She dressed slowly, closing her eyes to shut out the world which seemed so far away. In the kitchen, she made coffee. It was almost time for Oprah.

The first POP came from the bedroom. Another just beyond. Icy fright gripped her. Gunshots! Another POP. Coming closer. Then another. In panic Elizabeth dived behind the washing machine. Another POP sounded, echoing in the kitchen. Then all of a sudden, there were a series of automatic POPS. They went off all around her. Above her. Under her. Behind the Kenmore. She screamed, covering her ears, sucking in the acrid, fizzling smoke.

Firecrackers!

The blossoming gunmetal smoke mushroomed, filling the house with stink. Elizabeth was too petrified to move, so she didn't. She cried uncontrollably.

Ceasefire.

Then unexpectedly, another round went off. Elizabeth jumped with each POP. She jumped. And jumped.....and jumped. Then she cried some more.

Firecrackers!

Power is like having an orgy with yourself. Everything you do is viciously stimulating. I felt powerful, alive. I had that bitch pissing on herself.

"We're proud of you," Peters had said. "Keep up the pressure and soon she'll snap like a rotten pencil."

I believed it. I felt I could actually push someone to the brink of insanity. Now, that's control and I loved it. Now, I understood why white men could commit seeming atrocities and not think anything of it. Power confers power. Since the weak were without power, they were simply the conveniences of those who did possess it. You see, when you got juice, it ain't about right or wrong. It's about what's expedient. Get out of the way or get crushed. That should be the battle cry of every powerful person. It probably is. Motherfuckers just don't be saying it aloud.

This bitch. It was as though I could cover her heart with my hand and feel the terror in each throb. I can imagine her in bed asleep, her body thick with fear, so alive with dread that she can hardly rest. There is no refuge even in her dreams because I star in them. A leading man. She calls me the Ace-of-Spades man. I like that. Ace-of-Spades Man. It fits.

She is helpless against me. I am intimate with her, knowingly acquainted with her moods, her likes/dislikes; her hopes and fears. I have keys to her home. Her car. I decide shit for her. I push her towards madness.

I know how she feels because at no point during the entire course of my existence can I applaud myself for ever being happy. As a child, heartache came to nestle on my shoulders like a great falcon, plucking at my brains, devouring my pleasure center. I have grown fat on the bread of loneliness, supping from the cup of pain. Fear baby-sat me as a toddler, nourishing me with misery and cradling me from happiness. Then after a short session of abandon, put me under the direct care and supervisor of terror. I was, as a consequence, tutored in paranoia. I graduated, some time later, with a degree in suffering.

There is no hope for me. The best I can do is to beg for an unaccompanied stroll through the dead-end streets of my mind where I stand on the empty corner trying to make the light change. From red. To green. GO! It never works. The light in my mind is permanently stuck on red and this is where I remain, stalled at the fork in the road of my own life.

I stand there stupidly viewing what could have been, should have been, but opportunity is fluid, an impatient provider. Can't wait, won't. Is gone. The red light wouldn't change. I cry hot tears as I bear witness to the silent moan of beauty as it provides color commentary to everyone's life—but mine. I am stung by the neglect of not being invited to the banquet of life. I am simply a beggar, waiting on the light to change. A homeless vagabond with a bed of thorns.

This bitch. She is my pardon. I have to crush her. I have no choice. I will not flinch. The ball-squeezer has commissioned the act and I must comply because then and only then can I be free.

Red light. Bitch. Red light.

On Saturday, Elizabeth felt better so she went shopping. She wanted to upgrade her mood. The torrid grey sheets of rain had turned to a stringy, wet, misty drizzle and already she was feeling brighter. What would she buy? Shoes, most definitely. Perhaps, perfume. Something for the house. Not hardly.

It was good to feel good again. Shopping always lifted her up, so she leaned on the seat of the red Audi, feeling self-satisfaction oozing out of her pores. She was astonished that she could experience such warmth especially on such a gloomy day as this. She didn't dwell on the constant nightmare the other days and nights had been. She did not enjoy their recall. Instead, she focused on her upcoming shopping spree. A hat. Gloves. A coat. A bra for the Audi. She laughed. Why not? Just thinking in this fashion spread indiscriminate good cheer throughout her entire body.

At the SouthPark Mall, she gingerly picked her way through the dense throng of shoppers and all at once she felt eyes prickling her skin, piercing through her like shards of light. She paused for a moment in front of Saks Fifth Avenue. She drew back to stare into the window.

Then she saw him.

She stumbled backwards, bumping into an elderly couple, startling them. She apologized, floating away from them aimlessly. Her body, at once, felt flushed, hot to the touch, getting warmer. Her vision swirled, knees buckling, her weight unbearable upon them. He was behind her.

The Ace-of-Spades Man!

She spun around, glancing away from the reflection in the window. He was there, his eyes full of her. He waved.

Elizabeth's heart leaped. She started the journey towards him, but realized she didn't want to move. This close, from across the Mall, he appeared too strong, too powerful. She listened to the blood pounding against her temple and wanted help desperately. She turned to embrace a stranger—anyone—to beg for safety, but she felt her purse being snatched from her grip. A young boy was digging into it, wanting to steal.......Another boy approached from the right, tugging at her purse, opening it....No one tried to help. She broke away, running, looking over her shoulder.

The Ace-of-Spades Man was gone!

A heavy, dark weight descended upon her. She needed air. The EXIT beckoned and she pushed herself through it as fresh air slapped her face, whipping her alert. She ambled over to a stone bench, breathing fiercely, wanting to pump all the fear from her chest. Her leather handbag seemed to move against her body. She laid it beside her on the bench.

It moved! She was sure of it. She watched intently. Still dizzy from the shock of seeing the Ace-of Spades Man so close had dulled her senses, she told herself. Nothing was inside her handbag but--- it moved again. Squirmed.

Elizabeth moved away.

Out of the corner of her eye, she spotted the Mall's security van circling the perimeter. She flagged it down, bounding over to the curb. She tried to sound pleasant. "I know this may sound silly, but my handbag is alive."

"Huh?"

"No-no, Elizabeth stammered uncertainly. "I don't mean alive as you and I are alive, living and breathing....but it's moving."

"Maybe," the security guard joked, "the alligator wasn't all the way dead when they made that purse."

Elizabeth smiled weakly. "You see, it's cowhide."

"Maybe the cow came back to haunt you because you had his hide."

"Y-you don't believe me, do you?"

The security guard winked.

"Never mind," Elizabeth replied. "I don't know what came over me. I'm sorry."

Her handbag hadn't moved. It was still there. Harmless. She perched over it, lips pressed together quizzically. This was too much, she thought, sitting down, scooping up the handbag. She took two steps towards the parking lot, then stopped. Curiosity. What the hell, she told herself. *Take a peek.*

She flicked the gold clasp loose and peeked.

She screamed, tearing the handbag from her body, letting it drop.

Snakes　!

Her handbag was infested with them!

Tiny, Squirming. Ugly.

Then blackness swooped down upon her.

The deed was done. I had finished the bitch.

I needed no accolades, had no desire for the self-serving thunder of applause. The notice of my arrival had been served by the efficiency of my accomplished mission. Now I no longer had to pay lip service to my growing sense of power. Now, I had sufficient proof of it. But what now? Power is not a gilded toy that one trifles with on occasion nor is it a rich trinket to be seldom enjoyed. Nay, power is a sharp sword that begs to wallow in blood without let and I would not sheath mine. They should have known.

My power was too real, too endearing, too life-giving. I would not dismantle it. Were they fools? They should have known. They should have seen how much I had grown. They should have noticed the way I used my walk, so full of pomp and swagger, that I had become so much more than Eugene Larry, the damned. Everything about me virtually BOOMED with rejuvenation.

And that was why I had killed Peters!

I was hungry. They wouldn't give me the bitch and after bearing witness to my total mastery of her, tempting her close to death and then, at the very last possible moment, providing her with reprieve. It was such a sweet agony, but someone had to die.

And that was why I had killed Peters!

They had accorded me everything except the ability to play the final note, to strike that culminating chord.

And that was why I had killed Peters!

Somewhere Purple Haze was playing. Softly. So unlike the way it was meant to be played. Elizabeth could see nothing though. She was enslaved, it seemed, in a blinding wreath of lights that dazzled from a huge vaulted ceiling, mounted upon four thickly-padded walls.

She studied herself suspiciously. This was not her DKNY apparel. As a matter of fact, these were rough cotton pajamas. Why couldn't she release her arms from the sleeves of this-this-this strait-jacket!?

Purple Haze still softly whispered.

Where was she?

"Good Morning, Jane Doe."

Jane Doe, Elizabeth thought.

"How are you?"

Who me, Elizabeth wondered. Where was that voice coming from? She was alone.

"Don't worry," the kind voice said. "We will heal you."

Heal me? Am I ill? Elizabeth wondered.

The voice, ladylike and wonderful, melted into the ceiling.

Elizabeth pressed her back hard against the wall and using her legs like pistons pushed herself up until she was vertical. Height had the strange effect of expanding the unsettling experience of staring into a growling vortex that was trying to suck her into its' eye. She drank in the sensation.

She counted out a few disquieting steps. Stopped. Counted off a few disquieting heartbeats. Stopped. She continued to breathe slowly as she resumed her in-line breathing, trying to sense out what posed the greatest immediate threat to her.

"Good Morning," she shouted at the ceiling. "Hello."

A voice sounded through the void. "Yes, Jane Doe."

"My name is Elizabeth."

"Very well. What do you want?"

"Out."

"Out?"

"Yes, out of here. Out of these pajamas. Out of this." Elizabeth glared at the strait-jacket. "And once that is done, I'd like to know how I came to be-----". She paused. "Where am I anyway?"

"No need to worry yourself about anything, Jane Doe."

"Elizabeth. My.... name.... is.... ELIZABETH!"

"You won't accomplish much with that attitude," the voice said testily. "I urge you to remember that we are in charge and if you so much as attempt to cause problems during your stay here, then we have ways to make you fall in line."

Elizabeth's voice cracked. "I just want to go home. Is that too much to ask? I have a home. A life. I am somebody. I am Elizabeth Sellers and not some unknown Jane Doe. Please, let me go home."

"Now, listen here, young lady." It was a man's voice. Authoritative. "We cannot just let you go. You are mentally ill and you're here to be diagnosed and cured. You must be treated and I insist that you approach these therapy sessions with the view of helping us to help you as much as possible."

"But I don't need help."

"Good day, Jane Doe."

Elizabeth felt that her life had been sabotaged and that insanity did indeed circle above her, impairing her grasp of reality. She felt like a mechanized column of vertical cells, genes and chromosomes dipped in flesh, a chocolate shrine to something out of this world. She was definitely divorced from reality.

But where was she?

Baxter began to tremble..

The Senator was coming into the room. His breath quickened and he felt his stomach rumble. His bowels felt loose and he clasped his hands together to prevent them from trembling. This was crazy, he thought.

The Senator took a few hurried steps towards the parlor, sipping his drink and then turned around, leaving the heavy scent of his cologne hanging in the doorway.

"Be right with you," he yelled over his shoulder.

Baxter fumbled for a response, but remained mute. He heard a door close and wondered aloud. *What if he's on the phone and tells someone I'm here?* Baxter vacillated slightly, hyperventilating profusely. He'd better do this now. Get it over with.

He pulled the gun from under his jacket.

He clumsily crossed the room, the scent of cologne getting stronger. He reached for the door knob and in the same instant the door opened, the huge body of the Senator filling the entrance.

"W-what---?" Gaylord muttered before seeing the gun. "Put that thing up, Baxter."

Baxter raised the gun, pointing it at the Senator's torso.

Senator Gaylord stepped backwards into the den, his hands raised. "Baxter, dammit," he croaked between clenched teeth. "Let's talk."

"It's too late.'

"It's never too late." The Senator had moved into the center of the den.

Baxter slouched nervously in the doorway, gun hand shaking. "It's too late for me. It's too late for you. We're in this way too deep and there's no way out because you'll see to it that everyone sinks deeper until all of us are buried under your so-called vision."

"But we can win, Baxter. No one has too lose. Not us, anyway."

"You're no better than Hitler," Baxter spat. "You know that?"

"Look, killing me won't make whatever it is that's eating you go away, Baxter."

"Shut up," Baxter ordered. "Just shut the fuck up."

"Please, Baxter," the Senator pleaded, "don't do this. Don't do this, Baxter."

A thunderous growl started up from Baxter's gut, rising through his intestines, deepening to a howl that rippled violently through his chest, setting his entire body aflame. His eyes began to narrow, closing. The gun no longer sinister, now a red-hot exclamation point of his anger. His finger felt swollen, puffy, growing; forcing the trigger into motion. Then the metallic roar.

The thunderous noise jerked his eyes wide apart, compelling him to witness the bullet smash into the white shirt, tumbling the Senator over into an awkward, obscene sprawl. He yelled something unintelligible, clutching at the hole in his shirt, now oozing red. The Senator rolled over to his left side, sprinkling blood on the carpet, and propped himself on one knee. He shoved himself upward, reaching for the edge of the desk with crimson-stained fingers.

Baxter fired again. This bullet tore through Gaylord's shoulder, spinning him in a half-arc. He yelled again, swearing. Then, he collapsed.

Baxter lunged out of the doorway, running away. He tore at the front door and felt the cool night breeze wash his face. Was the Senator dead, he wondered? Had he killed him? He slammed his car into reverse and sped out of the driveway. Now what? Where did he go? Surely, not home.

It didn't matter much. His wife would find the note.

After about fifteen minutes of driving, he turned off the highway into an all night diner. He wanted a cup of strong, black coffee. He left the .357 Magnum in the car.

Once inside, he chose the largest Styrofoam cup available and filled it slowly, the rich steaming aroma wafting over him. At the last second before leaving the counter, he opted for two packets of sugar. Why not, he concluded. Live a little, he thought. After all, he had just killed a man.

Turning back onto the highway, he firmly tucked the coffee cup between his thighs and ripped the plastic lid off. The smell of dark, roasted coffee beans filled the car. He took a quick sip. Invigorating.

This was not at all like he imagined it would be although he declined to dwell upon the deed and he surely realized the mistake it would be to delve into the horror of what he still must do. Once he had cleared it with himself that there was no other way, he settled back, switching on the radio and resigned himself to his new life. It would be brief, but for once he could do exactly what he wanted. That was true freedom. He had lost his family so there was nothing else to venture.

He flung the coffee out of the window and with a sense of unrestrained glee watched the cup litter the highway. He tore off, speeding back onto the highway, spraying sand and rocks everywhere. Somehow this exorcised him, giving him unconcealed pleasure.

His beloved BMW gnawed viciously at the road, sprinting ahead, gaining on whatever was going to happen next. He passed one. Then another. They meant nothing to him and by the time he passed his third speed limit sign, he was doing in excess of 100 miles per hour.

Flashers!

It was the police. The whirling lights came up fast behind him, nudging him to go even faster. He let down the window to breathe in the howl of the squalling siren. He peeked into his rearview mirror. The police car was fast, approaching like heat, holding nothing back. Baxter suddenly felt uneasy about putting the trooper's life in danger. Perplexed, he slowed down. The poor bastard might have a family. Baxter slid off to the side of the road, braking the car. He waited.

The trooper was on the radio, requesting assistance. After a second, he approached the driver's side of the BMW, flashlight beaming, gun-holster unsnapped. His voice floated to Baxter. It was young and unsure.

"Step out of the car, please, and keep your hand where I can see them at all times."

Baxter stepped out of the car.

"Place your hands on the top of the car."

Baxter did as commanded.

The trooper quickly descended upon Baxter, frisking him roughly. Finding nothing, he scanned the interior of the vehicle. Seeing nothing, he relaxed. "Blowing off a little steam, eh?"

Baxter laughed mirthlessly. "That's pretty apt. I'll buy into that explanation if it suits your report."

"Where you coming from?"

"I always thought you guys asked for some identification first."

The trooper's casual mood vanished. "Gimme some ID and get back into your car while I run this through." He made to turn away. "And don't try nothing stupid."

Baxter slid back into the car and followed the cop's movement through his sideview mirror. He immediately felt the anxiety surface. He knew he wouldn't be able to dismiss it and there was no need to attempt to be level-headed. He didn't hesitate. He was not afraid.

The .357 sounded like a cannon.

"*Good God!*" the trooper hollered.

James Baxter slumped to the floor of his beloved BMW, wetting the dash with blood. He was dead.

For the first ten days, Elizabeth had lived in the padded cell, taking her food through a slot in the heavy iron door. She was escorted every day at precisely

2:30pm to a single shower stall at the end of a long, quiet hallway. Afterwards, sandwiched between the same pair of burly escorts, she would march back to her cell. She still didn't know where she was---exactly. She had been allowed no phone calls. No one could visit because no one knew where she was.

Today, she had an interview.

"Hello, Jane Doe," an emaciated white man offered. "How are you?"

The room was seemingly oval or maybe it was the fact that the chairs were arranged in a tight, gnarled circle. The room was peach-colored with sunshine blasting full upon the windows.

"Why do you----?" Elizabeth stopped. Her speech was slurred and thick. Her tongue was a flat and heavy pallet of flesh. "Why do you insist on referring to me as a Jane Doe? My name is Elizabeth Sellers. I imagine you have my credentials."

"I'm afraid we have no information on you and I'm equally afraid that you will have to remain an unofficial Jane Doe until there is concrete clarification of your identity."

"I just told you who I was."

"At any rate," the man said, ignoring her, "my name is Cole Aspin and I am the head administrator here at Glenwood Residential Treatment Center. Beside you on your left is Tracey Hamft, legal advisor. Next to her, you have Melissa Grady, a mental health specialist, and last but not least is Hank, a member of our security team." Aspin cleared his bony throat. "Now, that you're familiar with us, we'd like to get a bit more acquainted with you."

"I want to call someone," Elizabeth rasped, her throat dry.

"I'm sorry, but we have strict orders not to permit you any phone calls until---"

"Who ordered that?"

"Your sponsor."

"Sponsor?"

"We're not at liberty to divulge anything to you at this time. However your friend committed you personally and being that he is a person of some influence made it quite clear that your condition was indeed very serious. He also pointed out that your whereabouts should be kept secret." Aspin smiled. "All your family has been contacted." He smiled again. "They know you are being well cared for. Now," he slapped his knee, "let's conduct our utilization review, what do you say?" He leaned over and patted Elizabeth's hand. "We're going to move you out of the strip cell into a much better wing. You'll be able to watch tele---"

Elizabeth interrupted. "You've been drugging me, haven't you?"

Aspin shrugged. "Nothing more than a mild anti-depressant." He glanced at Melissa. "What is being administered?"

Melissa, a buxom brunette, scanned the chart. "A daily dose of Imipramine, 25 milligrams. The same of

Restoril, a mild sedative." She smacked her lips in finality. "Nothing else."

Elizabeth wanted to scream, could feel the force within her. Instead her voice was wounded. "You have drugged me against my will."

"All medications have been prescribed."

"Who prescribed me being held hostage?"

"Once more, Miss Jane Doe," Aspin countered, "the purpose of this review is not designed for you to engage us in destructive verbal attacks. Understand? We are here to assess your adjustment reaction and in so doing maybe establish some relevant guidelines to expedite your recovery and subsequent release. We will require," he said threateningly, "your fullest cooperation. I assure you that you do not wish to have a disorderly conduct demerit on your record."

Hank snickered.

During the initial phase of the review, Aspin tendered neutral questions that left open the possibility that Elizabeth was indeed a Jane Doe although she was convinced that this was unlikely. They knew who she was. Someone was paying them or pressuring them to act as though they didn't.

"Do you recall the date of your admission here?"

Elizabeth did not.

"Do you recall the chain of events that led to your admission here?"

Elizabeth did not.

Her uneasiness blew up, magnifying itself. They were sizing her up and she was giving a piss-poor account of herself. If she was not able to persuade them, then there was no telling what they might do. Suddenly, for the first time, she thought of the Ace-of-Spades Man. Was he alone liable for her predicament? What about Ronpis? Who was Ronpis?

"You are still acutely disoriented. I am going to refer you to bi-weekly sessions of milieu therapy."

"And what of a phone call?" Elizabeth asked Aspin.

"The sessions are merely educational," he continued as if Elizabeth had not spoken. "I feel you will derive great benefit from them. Then at some point, we might consider scheduling family sessions for you."

"Are any of you familiar with the Safety Pins Day Care Center case?"

Aspin spoke. "I believe you refer to the trial where the day care facility was ordered closed----"

"Well," Melissa interrupted, "it didn't stay closed long. The judge just issued an Order reopening it."

"What?!" Elizabeth exclaimed. "That can't be. You see, I'm the------"

"I'm sorry, Miss Doe," Aspin revealed, "but if you excite yourself I'll simply have to terminate this appointment and recommit you to the strip cell. And there you won't have even the slightest chance of securing a phone call." He sighed. "Let us pose the questions, please?"

The second phase of the interview went as badly as the first and Elizabeth knew it. She glanced at the others seated in the circle trying to read a verdict in their expressions. Unexpectedly, Aspin stood up and motioned for Tracey Hamfpt to accompany him to a distant window outside the circle. The others remained seated, neither speaking nor smiling. The private conversation was brief.

"We're moving you to a less restrictive wing in the facility."

"Is there, will there be a phone?"

"No. Not yet, Miss Doe."

"B-but," Elizabeth sobbed, "I need to make a phone call."

Aspin nodded to Hank.

"Let's go," Hank barked unkindly.

Three days later. Sunday.

Elizabeth saw the mustard-colored girl sitting at the back of the television room with her head down as if she were praying. Elizabeth looked over the room. There were no other blacks there. Elizabeth moved towards the back, squeezing down the aisle, heading in the direction of the girl. Elizabeth walked past. The girl didn't glance up. Elizabeth studied her from a distance then moved through the chairs, sitting down beside her.

The mustard-colored girl offered no greeting, no acknowledgment that someone was sitting next to her.

Elizabeth remained seated, but said nothing until the hall monitor, a masculine-looking white female, was out of ear-shot.

"Hello, my name is Elizabeth. What's yours?"

The girl said nothing aloud although Elizabeth could clearly see her lips moving fervently. Prayer?

"Hello," Elizabeth persisted. "What is your name?"

Exposed to sound, the mustard-colored girl's lips moved faster, her eyes clenched even more tightly.

Elizabeth reached out, forcibly shaking the girl's knee. "I am a friend."

"QUIET!" the manly woman screeched. "*SSSSHHH!*"

The girl appeared very unhappy with the interruptions, but still Elizabeth wasn't satisfied with her unresponsiveness. She took a deep breath and watching for the hall monitor reached over and pinched the girl's arm brutally. The girl offered no resistance. She indicated her displeasure by praying aloud.

"Dear Lord," the mustard-colored girl chanted, "don't let them give us any more green jello and please let them take away the spoiled milk at breakfast. Please let the monsters in my head go to sleep when I do, so they won't mess with me while I'm dreaming....."

"Oh God." Elizabeth moaned. "I'll never get her attention."

The mustard-colored girl's divine petition got louder and longer until in passing she caught the notice of the hall monitor. Elizabeth scooted down two seats and pretended to watch Jeopardy. The woman on the show had just wagered all her money except a dollar.

Ingrid, the hall monitor, was stooped over saying something to the girl. After a second, the prayers ceased and Ingrid smiled graciously, whipping out a miniature Tootsie Roll and dropping in the upturned, outstretched hand of the girl.

Ingrid stared at Elizabeth. "Were you bothering her?"

"No."

"Then, don't," Ingrid said before storming off, bumping into a chair. When she got to the end of the row, she turned to face Elizabeth. Ingrid smiled and flipped a Tootsie Roll through the air. Elizabeth caught it clumsily. She started to smile, but it was too late. Ingrid had gone.

Elizabeth hurriedly moved back down the chairs until she was once more beside the girl. She tossed the piece of candy into the girl's lap. "God sent me," she whispered before moving away.

The girl looked up quickly, seemingly pleased.

"I'll see you tomorrow," Elizabeth promised.

The next day, the mustard-colored girl scoffed at tradition. She didn't rush immediately to the back of the TV room when viewing hours began. Instead, she waited at the door counting people until Elizabeth entered. She moved silently behind Elizabeth and tugged anxiously at her sleeve.

"Did God really send you?"

Using all the persuasiveness she could muster, Elizabeth whispered that she had indeed been commissioned by God to check on her. The mustard-colored girl appeared transfixed by this news, but after a second or two seemed to recede to another dimension in her outlook. She grew quiet.

"What is my name?"

"Let's sit down first." Elizabeth stalled.

"*What is my name!?*" the girl asked again, more persistent this time.

"Is it that important?"

"Yes"

"Why?"

The girl was visibly disappointed. "You mean God sent you and He didn't even tell you my name?" She started to cry. "Does He think my name is Jane Doe, too?" She wiped away a tear. "Nothing is wrong with me."

"In ten minutes," Ingrid instructed, "all conversation must cease."

"Do you want out of here?"

The question evidently involved thought since Elizabeth didn't get a quick response. The girl pondered it for longer than suited Elizabeth so she reminded the girl that being locked away was not wanted God wanted for any of His creatures and that it was not wrong for them to stand up for their freedom. "We have to choose," Elizabeth contended. "And when we have done all that we can do, then God will do the rest. But if we do nothing, then He will do nothing."

"If I had to choose," the girl said," I would want to be home. Yeah," she sobbed, "that would be nice."

"Listen closely. Do you have phone privileges?"

"Uh-huh."

"I'm going to give you a telephone number-------"

"QUIET!" Ingrid commanded. "Television is on."

".....And I want you to read---"

"QUIET!"

".....What is written on the paper to them. Understand?"

"QUIET!"

"And we'll get out just like that?'

"That's right."

"I'll do it. I'll do it," the girl beamed. "Pass me the note. I'll do it. I'll do it."

Elizabeth's eyes held the girl's. "It will be all over soon. Trust me."

No longer feeling helpless, Elizabeth's spirit soared. She settled back, staring vacantly at the tube. Oprah was on. She liked Oprah and was better able to enjoy the show. Since she was now allowed to go to the dining room, there was no way they could lace her food with drugs so everything now resounded with sharper clarity. She was glad of that and prayed there would be no adverse side effects that she would have to deal with in the future.

At that moment something funny happened on the television and everyone laughed including the mustard-colored girl. For no apparent reason, Elizabeth joined in the infectious commotion. God, it felt good to laugh.

During a commercial break, she went for a drink of water. Someone, Ingrid, more than likely, had left the local section of a week old newspaper on the counter. Curiously, Elizabeth flipped it open, thumbing through it quickly before Ingrid could catch her and rip the paper from her hands. Her eyes went to work swiftly, scanning the columns, the boxes, the headlines. She saw nothing about her. Her heart sank. She turned the paper over on its back and instantly the bold type stole her attention. She gobbled up the news greedily and as Ingrid approached, took another sip of the cold fountain water.

She scrambled back to her seat, wondering why anyone would want to shoot Senator Gaylord. He had seemed so pleasant that evening at her home. After all, he had been the one who had given her the tickets to Hawaii even though the Ace-of-Spades man had ruined the vacation.

At least, she sighed, the Senator was still alive.

Shortly past midnight, the door to her room was snatched open forcefully and before she could wipe the sleep from her eyes, they were swiftly upon her, swarming her cot like angry bees.

"That's her. That's her," the mustard-colored girl shouted gleefully. "I told you I knew what I was talking about. See," she pointed. "That's her. That's her."

"Need I say how much you have disappointed us all," Aspin cackled, his Adam's apple bobbing up and down. "You leave me no choice." He stepped out of the room with his arm draped protectively over the shoulder of the mustard-colored girl. "Okay, Hank," he said.

"Can I have my Tootsie Rolls now?"

Elizabeth heard the mustard-colored girl begging for candy just before the four male orderlies did a take-down on her, pinning her to the mattress and injecting her with Thorazine.

"On the count of three," Hank barked. "One...two...three"

Lifting mattress and all, the four men returned Elizabeth back to the padded cell.

Elizabeth had to squeeze information from her head. What day was it? When was the last time she had eaten? Where were all her friends?

In a sort of befuddled daze, she haphazardly examined those facts and realized that she had no answers. All she could hope to do in her present condition was to attempt to interest herself in finding out more about herself, her whereabouts, her life. There were times of fuzzy incoherence when she did not care, but these periods were interspersed with moments of silent lucidity when she experienced a strong desire to be....somewhere else.

The tranquilizers made her feel as if she was melting, the skin unnaturally seeping off her bones, dripping into a chocolate mound on the floor. Her heart beat had no cadence, no rhythm as her heart simply worked to keep her alive. It purposely toiled with efficiency, but without urgency. She slipped into the void.

Inside the vacuum, Elizabeth's eyeballs felt heavy, boring life-sized holes into the thick walls, but every time she turned her head ever so slightly, the holes would disappear before she could get up to push her body through. This happened a half-dozen times and no longer able to mask her irritation, she screwed up her face into a tight ball and cried. After the first seven tears, the salty stream turned wooden, illegitimate. She dried her eyes. Turned inward. Tried to conceal something from herself and wondered what it was.

Suddenly, the big door clanged open. The big shadow turned into Ingrid. "So," she retorted playfully, "you like getting into trouble?"

Elizabeth didn't answer the question. She posed one of her own. "What do you want?"

"To help you, if possible." Ingrid kept her voice low.

"Help? How?" Then. "Why?"

Ingrid glanced nervously out into the hallway. "You don't deserve to be here. You still want help, don't you?" She brandished a set of keys tauntingly. "Don't you still want out of here?"

"Can you help me? Will you?" Elizabeth was pleading.

Ingrid's rugged features turned jello soft. "I might," she whispered, "because I know you don't belong in here, but that ain't why I'll help you." She pointed at Elizabeth's hand. "I want that rock."

Elizabeth absently stared at the modest diamond ring the senior partners at her law firm had given her as a gift after winning the Safety Pins case. "This?"

"Yes. That."

Elizabeth fell silent.

Ingrid glanced into the hallway once more. "Look, dearie. It's not like you've got much of a choice if you want my help, and given your predicament, I'm being more than fair. I could take the damn ring," she hissed, "and leave you here to forever piss in a hole in the floor." She stepped closer, talking softly. "I really want that ring and I'm trying to earn it, so now the choice is yours." She stood tall. "I'm leaving with your ring. Whether you get something in return or not depends on you." She then turned menacing, thrusting out her hand. "Gimme the rock."

Elizabeth folded her arms defiantly across her chest.

"Gimme that phone number and I'll contact your friends, let them know where you are. I promise."

Elizabeth's strength faded. Slowly, she removed the ring. Hopeful. "Please," she moaned before dropping the ring into Ingrid's outstretched palm. "Please," she repeated. "Help me."

Ingrid spun around and left, saying nothing.

Cole Aspin slammed the phone down hard. Then he started barking orders in rapid-fire succession that instantly turned the usual tranquil Glenwood Center into a frenzy of bee-hive activity.

At first, to Ingrid, it seemed all so patently ridiculous with people bumping into each other or trying to talk with their mouths full of doughnuts, the white sugary powder frosting their moving lips like snow on the side of a mountain. She was the only one who knew or had any idea what had prompted the busy-as-a-bee commotion. A tiny laugh settled amicably in her throat as Hank grabbed her by the arm, tugging her towards the door.

"Bring the car around to the back exit," Hank announced excitedly. "Hurry up," he ordered. "Leave it running and then get missing." He shoved her towards the parking lot. "Move it," he snarled before dashing back inside the building.

Ingrid was in no hurry. She gazed across the parking lot into the sunshine flickering off The Holiday Day Inn sign. Heads were going to roll, she assumed. She had already rehearsed her lines in case anyone wanted to question her. *I was just following orders,* she would say. That should be defense enough. If not, she could always invoke the Fifth Amendment. Court TV had taught her that much.

Just before getting into the Center's program car, she briefly stood shrouded, frozen in heroic balm. For once, she had just maybe done the right thing, and plus had gotten a big, fat diamond ring in the process. She threw her head back and laughed wildly.

Inside the padded cell, Elizabeth was on her feet. The heavy, iron door was flung open, banging loudly into the outer wall. Elizabeth shrieked. They engulfed her like a cloud, two tugging forcefully at her ankles, one pushing her over, two waiting to break her backward sprawl by gripping her arms. Just like that she was stretched taut, carried prone by four burly male security officers. She tried to struggle, to resist, but it was useless. They had her. Down the hall they ran with her body vicariously spread-eagled in their grasp.

Aspin stepped quickly out of an office. "Here's her file. "He thrust the folder at Hank.

Before Elizabeth knew it, Melissa Grady had jabbed her in the arm, pumping her full of medication. Almost instantly, Elizabeth's body sagged, dangling in the air like a deflated brown balloon.

"Noooo," she remembered saying.

Out back, the car was waiting. The back door was opened and Elizabeth was pitched in. She was drooling, long lines of glistening saliva forming on her chin, dripping onto her shoulder.

"They'll know what to do once you get there," Aspin consoled Hank. "Call me as soon as you---"

The sound of Aspin's voice became lost in the raucous shrill of police sirens as four squad cars barreled around the building, zeroing into the parking lot, hemming the brown Mercury in.

Everyone froze in place.

George Bailey leaped from the doorway of his car and raced over to the Mercury, peeking in. "Here she is," he shouted angrily. "She's in the back seat." Two officers ran over. "That's her," Bailey pointed. "That's Elizabeth Sellers." He reached in, cradling her head in his arms, the tears flowing. "My God," he groaned. "What have they done to her?"

The officers slowly extricated the limp, unconscious body from the car. She hung limply in their grasp, her head bobbing precariously on her shoulders, her frail frame sunk into a sad pathetic lump of upturned flesh. Around her tired, closed eyes were deep ringed ridges of swollen, puffy blackness while her lips, clamped shut, were cracked and dry, the skin peeled back like parched fish scales .

"We better get her to a hospital," one of the officers mentioned to Bailey. "You can follow us and make sure she gets checked in properly."

Bailey rushed back to his Lincoln Continental. He flung an angry fist at Hank and the others. "You animals will pay for this," he snarled. "I'll see to that."

He cried all the way to the hospital.

That night they met at The Blue Marlin Restaurant for dinner and drinks, celebrating the Senator's recovery. Everyone ordered drinks early and fussed over the Senator's comfort to the point where it made him self-conscious.

"Hell, boys, I'm no invalid," Senator Gaylord exclaimed, "and according to all the doctors and nurses," he winked slyly, "I should be ditching this contraption soon." He patted the arms of the wheelchair.

Actually Gaylord basked in the attention, but it bordered a little too much on the side of sympathy and not enough towards the fear he used to elicit from them. He felt it was due time he restored the balance. It was time to bring the men back in full contact with his total mastery over them. What they needed, Gaylord reckoned, was a refresher course in fear and terror.

The Senator's sunken features contained a number of contradictions. One side of his face seemed paler than the other, the darker side bowed out at the nose and cheeks meeting his mouth like an upside down fruit bowl. His neck appeared to be perforated with a dozen or so welt-red creases that formed maddeningly circled loops similar to those age rings etched into the stumps of a tree. The Hermes silk scarf hid most of those nicely.

"You look so unhappy," the Senator chided Torrence. "Thought I was trying to weasel out of my obligations by stopping two bullets." He laughed. "Hell, it will take a lot more than a bee-stinger like a .357 to put me out of commission."

"I still can't get over Baxter," August Overton piped in. "I never would have figured him to be a...." His voice trailed.

"Sometimes," The Senator admonished, "it is impossible to read a man's script, so I'm not that amazed. That's why, gentlemen, we can't get consumed by the small details of what we do. It's the big picture that must drive us or else we all could make a career-ending choice."

"Hell, Senator, you speak as though Baxter merely lost his job. Jesus, the man is dead." Baldwin gulped his drink. Looked away.

The Senator looked astonished. He smirked. "Life routinely gets lost in the shuffle of our every day affairs and we have no immunity from death's decree, so why sweat it. It's small stuff. While a man breathes, he is defined by his career and he should fight tooth and nail to preserve it. To be held accountable is the mark of distinction to which we must all subscribe." After taking a sip from his drink, he smiled approvingly at McManus. "I studied your annual report. I like what's evolving, but", he quipped, "rid your puppet of his cigarette smoking habit at once. Don't want to do anything to damage the lil' booger's respiratory system, especially if, as you contend in your report, to have him ready to start producing children at thirteen." Gaylord winked. "Got to have wind in his sails to produce in conformity with your projections."

"Yes sir," McManus replied meekly.

Noticing the pained expression on McManus' face, the Senator chortled. "Tell us about the plans for your puppet."

"Actually, it's nothing."

"He explains it as nothing," the Senator deadpanned. "Nothing short of revolutionary is what he means. My opinion is that he is going to make himself very, very wealthy by marketing his own line of puppets and since he was the first one to get the idea on paper, none of you can steal it. The idea is his and is as good as patented, so gentlemen, if you will, let's honor our esteemed colleague with a rousing round of applause for being the first charter member to trademark a great idea"

The men clapped and cheered.

"Speech. Speech," someone chanted, egging McManus on. "Speech."

"Okay," McManus relented. "Alright." He sipped his drink. "It's no big deal really, and given Baldwin's Freudian background, I'm surprised he didn't beat me to the punch. After all, I just drew upon the sexual propensity of blacks and their penchant for having babies at an early age, so I figured out how to capitalize on this phenomenon. I intend to transform my puppet into a stud. I propose to have William siring at least three children a year once he's sperm-ready and all of these children I will personally farm out to others. It is my hope to biologically reduce the prep time of these puppets through the inherent genetic chemistry of William, their father. I intend to genetically reverse Darwin to the point where only William's recessive genes will be transferred to his offspring, rendering them more susceptible to instruction. In essence, I want them, in a manner of speaking, cable-ready right out of the womb."

"But suppose ol' Willie Boy is impotent?" someone asked.

"Or if he's not impotent, who's to say he won't produce only girls?" another quizzed.

Senator Gaylord motioned for silence. "One question at a time. Give him time to answer."

"Regarding the first question," McManus queried, "he's fine. I have already had him inspected and barring some injury, he should have a healthy sperm count. As he grows older, I'll get him involved in lifting weights and staying in shape. This will help boost his sperm output." He grinned. "And as for his producing males or females, he will know, believe me, the value of siring strong, healthy boys. As a matter of fact, there is presently a lot of literature available that graphically details the sexual hows, whens and whats of producing males."

"So you intend to manufacture---?"

"A more pliant product," McManus conceded. "With the field of genetic engineering expanding as it currently is, I don't envision there being a problem with instilling in newborn puppets, genes that inculcate submissiveness. If this proves accurate as I'm sure it will, I will be able to offer a puppet far improved than the ones currently available by lottery, but," he chuckled, "technology costs, so bring your checkbooks."

"Okay," the Senator announced, "that's enough shop talk for the moment. Let's eat, drink, and be merry."

Elizabeth spent most of the next week cooped up in the hospital. That's how she felt. Caged. It was, however, a less confining sensation than what she had experienced at Glenwood. As time passed, she awkwardly got stronger and began moving about through the long, clean corridors, acknowledging courtesies and speaking directly to strangers, learning to trust again. She was making progress.

The aftereffects of the drugs had worn off long before the muted memories of Glenwood. They still both numbed her and chilled her. She was still prone to uncontrollable crying at which time her blood would boil and she'd economize this anger by concentrating on the Ace-of-Spades Man. He was a real villain.

Her constant companion during this time was her friend April, who sat with her every day, chatting her up about everything. It was April who had managed to fill the trunk of her Toyota Celica with stacks of newspapers. These were the September 1st editions from various and sundry cities across the nation that dated back as far as 1940.

September 1st.

That date meant something. Otherwise it wouldn't keep coming up.

Initially, April had playfully dismissed her "9-1" conspiracy theory as she had dubbed it, content to listen for a brief while and then tactfully changing the subject. Now, however, there were longer thoughtful silences when Elizabeth would stare into space and ask her friend. *"Doesn't that strike you as strange?"* or" *Don't you feel that something is happening with this?"* These vague, subtle shifts in April's responses pushed

Elizabeth's hopes up because if she could persuade April, the die-hard-show-me-the-proof pessimist, then she was onto something significant. However, even with April's coming aboard, more concrete evidence would have to be gathered before any giant steps could be taken.

During the rest of her stay at Carolinas Medical, usually long after April had gone for the evening, she would appoint herself as legal custodian of her fears and then pray she would find Ronpis before it did some appointing of its own. It would be, she clearly recognized, an appointment with death. *Hers.* The Ace-of-Spades Man would come calling.

September 1st?

What did it mean?

Somehow this date had become a personal liability to young, black boys, but what did it mean? This was becoming the most bewildering question of her life and for once the weight of her brilliance had provided no extensive breakthroughs. She was halted dead in her tracks and it filled her with disgust because she recognized with certainty that she didn't know what she was searching for. Sometimes her opinions held merit. At other times, they couldn't hold water. It was such an undignified way to save black boys who now she felt were in grave peril----from something.

Ronpis?

The Ace-of-Spades Man?

Her own paranoia

When Elizabeth got out of the hospital, April decided it was time to organize a "reading party". She had just finished reading the Pittsburg Courier's September 1st, 1948 edition. The Courier was one of the oldest black newspapers in print at the time and after a point-by-point examination of some of the things she had read, some things never changed. Black women, she noted, had always been the lowest paid wage-earner since blacks were allowed into the marketplace. Even now, they were at the bottom of the wage-earning totem pole.

"Look at this," Gail Brown commented, referring to a September 1st editorial in The Atlanta Constitution. "The teen birthrate among our women is the highest ever and it goes on to say that these teenaged sistas are more than likely to be a victim of a violent crime in greater numbers than anyone else except black, teenage boys."

"The Virginia Ledger," Henrietta Johnson interjected woefully, "adds that in 1996, the AIDS rates for sistas is eighteen times that of white women."

Elizabeth was pulled from her search by April. "Didn't you say that Eugene Larry was born September 1st 1962?"

"Umm-hmm," Elizabeth mumbled, becoming alert. "Find something?"

"Just the opposite," April remarked apologetically. "Nothing happened on that day in this newspaper from Florida. Nothing."

Evident dismay crossed Elizabeth's face. "I thought maybe...Never mind," she concluded.

"Do not assume defeat, sista," Lisa instructed bravely. "I agree with your theory and if anything is to be found, the Carolina Association of Black Women Entrepreneurs will find it." She saluted. "We have a reputation to uphold. Don't worry. If's it here, we'll know it. We'll find it."

"I'm just amazed that nothing has turned up yet," Elizabeth groaned. "It seems like we've been here for days already."

"Four hours, thirty five minutes," Henrietta laughed, looking at her watch. She stood and stretched. "It's not like we've wasted time, but we may have to become a little more systematic on our next round through this," she pointed, "ton of paper. We have got to devise a system or else we'll soon be struggling against fatigue and bound to miss something. This is not simply a case of trying to look up a birthday----"

"Or an obituary," Gail included.

"We must be more specific," Henrietta challenged. "I hate sports and besides being bored to death by reading all the scores and who did what, I wouldn't know what in the world to even begin looking for. Me. I like browsing through the locals. I'm less likely to get bored. Someone else can please do the sports. I don't know a touchdown from a......" her voice ended. "Told you," she shrugged. "Let me at the local section."

"That may be a good idea," April considered. "Let's divide the papers into sections and everybody can chose a category. "I'll take sports."

"First, let's take five," Elizabeth suggested.

"Since you like the locals so much," Gail insisted to Henrietta, "you can finish reading about this ancient murder in California. My Mama wasn't even born in 1952, and honey I ain't wanting to read nothing older than my Mama."

The women laughed.

Henrietta took the paper and placed it face down, then decided to peek at the article. "Hmmph," she snorted, laying the article back down. "Dumb ol' black men can't get enough of white women. This is the same ol' story."

"What happened?" April asked.

"Nigga in California raped this white woman named Gaylord and----"

"*Named what?!*" Elizabeth exploded, visibly excited. "What did you say?"

Henrietta picked the paper up. "Eunice Gaylord was the woman's name. Was raped and killed the papers say."

Elizabeth tugged, demanding the paper. Henrietta let it go, but all the women gathered around, fueled by Elizabeth's interest.

"What is it? What is it?" Lisa gasped.

"Shhh. Shhh," April cautioned. "Let her read....Let us pray."

Elizabeth's wide-opened eyes moved rapidly over the text, giving no thought to the women crowded close at her elbow. At the end of the article, her eyes raced once more to the top, consuming the words a second time. Halfway through, she grew uncomfortable with the internal suggestion that this could be something. She squeezed her eyes shut, sealing in darkness, lamely disrupting the blur of black/white newsprint. Her heart raced. Thumping. And then going BOOM. After a brief second, she opened her eyes, feeling vaguely silly. "It's probably nothing," she finally croaked.

No one believed her. The air was too electrified.

"Don't lie too us, girl," April begged. "This is it," she pointed. "Or you wouldn't have turned two shades lighter if it wasn't. Girl, this is a touchdown, isn't it?"

Elizabeth fell back into her chair, her chest heaving hard. "I don't know exactly," she sighed in exasperation, "but we'll know in a minute."

"The Gaylord woman," Henrietta whispered. "She is what this is all about, isn't she?"

Elizabeth was afraid to speak and for a while, she didn't. When she did, her voice sounded raspy. "All I can say is that I know a Gaylord, a Senator. He mysteriously showed up the night Lou and Sandra threw me a celebration party after the Safety Pins case." She drew a big breath, taking the air in slowly. "Although he and Sandra knew each other professionally, there had never been a personal friendship. A few times, Sandra herself remarked about her surprise at the Senator just popping up that night. Later that same night, she mentioned in passing that the Senator was raised in Sacramento."

Where the Gaylord woman was raped and killed?"

"Yes," Elizabeth managed to say. "It may mean nothing. They are literally thousands of people with that last name. It may mean nothing," Elizabeth croaked. "Nothing at all. Do you all hear me?" Her voice cracked.

"Don't get emotional on us now, Miss Lady," April cracked. "If this is it, then you have got to face it or you won't make it. I can guarantee that much. If it's as big as you think it is, then it will destroy black women with the same lack of compassion it reserves for black men."

"If this is it," Gail added, "it's time to go to war."

"Let's go." The women followed Elizabeth into the spacious study where she plopped down in front of the computer, cautiously activating the machine. A tiny shiver crept up her spine, chilling her. The women gathered around, hushed, filling the room with intense expectancy. The computer whirred consolingly as Elizabeth peeked over her shoulder into anxious faces.

"Go ahead, Elizabeth," April commanded firmly.

Immediately, Elizabeth entered cyberspace, clicking over to a web search engine, HotBot, and deftly typed in J-U-N-I-U-S-G-A-Y-L-O-R-D. Without delay, a page popped up. The women hawked the page.

As a single unit, they ignored the birthdate. They skipped over the home address. They paid no attention to the social security number. The phone number was of no consequence. They rolled their eyes over the names of the children.....then EUREKA! Gaylord's mother's name was Eunice!

Elizabeth broke down. She wept.

They met at The House of Prayer Restaurant on Beatties Ford Road, and after the drama of the day before, Elizabeth was glad to settle into the relative ease of the next day. The sun had arrived and was shining brightly in a warming day-glo dazzle.

Both Elizabeth and Lou sat hunched over a home-cooked meal, the inviting scent of the food lingering in the air. Between bites of fish, the conversation went back and forth innocently for about ten minutes.

"So what do you think?" Lou finally asked

"I'd bet my life that the connections fit between Gaylord and Jenners."

Lou smiled. "They do. I did some deep digging into Jenners' background and as luck would have it, I learned that he and Gaylord went to college together. UCLA. They both left school at the same time."

"But do you believe that the death of Gaylord's mother on September 1st is the key to solving this puzzle?" Elizabeth shrugged. "It sure would answer a lot of questions if it was since everything seems to hinge on that date. Eunice Gaylord was raped and murdered on that day. Exactly ten years later, Eugene Larry was born on that date. And a generation later, "the boys" were all born. Sure makes you wonder"

"And who can forget," Lou added, "that September 1st was the day chosen for Safety Pins' grand opening when it first came on the scene? From the looks of it, Gaylord has a vendetta against black males born of September 1st, the anniversary of his Mama's death."

"But why here in Charlotte?"

"I think I have an answer for that," Lou grinned. "Gaylord attended UNC-Charlotte for a while before be went back out West to enroll at UCLA. Now, get this, he was in Charlotte when Eugene Larry was born."

"But how would a newborn black baby boy figure in all of this?"

"I don't know exactly.....yet, but I do know that it also involves the prison/industrial complex." Lou gestured. I did some more snooping into my hunch about Ronpis and CEA and I finally got a face for the Correctional Enterprises of America."

"You did? Who?"

"A dude from Alaska named Harris Ryan. Eskimo. Megarich. Anyway, what he is into is prisons. He is either buying them or building them. He's making a killing, but in order for his business to prosper, he has to have healthy bodies in the beds, follow what I'm saying? If Ryan builds a prison, he expects to have them filled."

"OMG!" Elizabeth exclaimed.

"Now, you getting the picture, I see. Prisons for profit. It's all the rage these days. Owning a professional sports team is so yesterday because nothing on the planet can make a hustler richer than owing a prison. Look at the news. All those young brothas that you see in handcuffs only make guys like Ryan richer because as long as there is crime, CEA can't go wrong." Lou wiped his mouth. "And guess who else is a partner-in-crime with Ryan? Ol' Gaylord."

"It's all beginning to make sense now. Gaylord is the monster I've been looking for."

Lou reached into his jacket pocket. "Now, I have something for you to feast your eyes on." He withdrew his hand slowly. The hand continued to move dramatically slow, inching towards Elizabeth, palm downward. Elizabeth giggled like a school-girl. "Now, tell me, my friend, if you recognize the star of this glamour shot. BAM!" He flashed the mug-shot under Elizabeth's nose.

Elizabeth took a single glance........and fainted.

Lou rushed around the table too her, the question already solved.

Eugene Larry. The Ace-of-Spades Man. The same

The insistent ring was distinct. Her Ringmaster. No one used that number----except her parents. Elizabeth jumped back. Startled. She stared meanly at the phone. The Ace-of Spades Man, no doubt. She would ignore it, just let it ring. Sooner or later, he would get the message. She walked away. The ringing stopped.

It started again.

Trembling, Elizabeth left the room. After a few seconds, the noise ceased.

"Fuck you, Eugene Larry, you Ace-of-Spades bastard."

On the wall. In the kitchen. The phone. It was buzzing with the distinctive ring. Two can play this game, she decided. She picked up the receiver, severing the connection, then put the receiver back.

Silence. Then abruptly.

RIING!

Again, she lifted the receiver, restoring quiet to the house.

RIING!

"This has gone too damn far," Elizabeth shrieked. For a moment, she glared at the wall phone, frightened, dry-mouthed. Trembling, she gathered her nerves and yanked up the receiver. "Listen, you criminal. I'll call---"

"Elizabeth! Elizabeth!" a familiar voice thundered in her ear. "What's going on?"

"Mr. Bailey," Elizabeth wailed sheepishly. "I'm very sorry. I thought you---"

"No need to explain. Are you okay....? You're sure...? Okay, then I'm holding you to that promise." There was a muffled pause. "Alright, here it is." He gave her a local telephone number. "Call. Ask for Theresa Baxter. It is very important from what she says. She sounds sincere, Elizabeth. Says it is imperative that she get in touch with you."

"Did she, by and chance, explain the urgency?'

"No. She insisted it was for your ears only. She simply said she knew."

"Knew what?"

"You've got the number. Make the call and see."

When she hung up the phone, Elizabeth studied the number. 704-123-9846. The name, Theresa Baxter, was as strange as the number. What could this stranger at this strange number know? She quickly picked up the phone. Now was as good a time as any to find out.

The phone was answered at once.

"Hello" It was a breathless voice. Female.

"This is Elizabeth Sellers. I'd like to speak with a Mrs. Theresa Baxter."

"Miss Sellers, thank God," the voice gasped. "I'm Theresa Baxter."

"Good. Now what is it that you know?"

"Not over the phone. Can we meet somewhere?"

Elizabeth was thinking.

"Please," Theresa Baxter begged. "You need to know this."

"Listen, Mrs. Baxter, I'll be candid with you. I've been through a lot recently and I have had to deal with some weird, insane people of both sexes and right now, I'm not too thrilled at the prospect of meeting with some stranger in reference to who-in-the-world-knows-what."

"Please, this is vital too you."

"How's this? I'll give you about fifteen seconds to interest me." Elizabeth peeked at her watch. "Fair enough?"

The husky, breathless voice didn't hesitate. "Senator Gaylord....Safety Pins Day Care Center....Ronpis.....Eugene Larry."

"Now it was Elizabeth's turn. She didn't flinch. "My office.....Right now.....Come quick!"

Elizabeth felt perspiration on her brow and her hands trembled slightly. She stared out of the window again for about the sixth time. It was something to do since sitting still was not a possibility. The sky had on a winter's coat, old-looking and faded grey, but it was not chilly. Just a blue-grey pale, early hint of what was to come.

From behind her, a soft knock. She hurriedly strode across the office, opening the door.

"Mrs. Baxter?"

"Yes, I'm Theresa Baxter."

"Please come in."

The women sat facing each other across Elizabeth's desk. They measured each other, dismissing all formalities, offering no pleasantries. Theresa reached into a briefcase, her husband's, and arranged a thin sheath of papers, a personal diary, and a manila envelope in front of her. This done, she carefully appraised the arrangement for exactness as if they were courtroom exhibits. Satisfied, she clasped her hands together prayerfully and spoke in her husky, breathless manner.

"It would be better if I start at the beginning, but I don't know where that is, so I'll just start where I came in."

"Which was?"

"The night my husband," Theresa Baxter lowered her eyes, "killed himself. It was also the night he tried to kill Senator Gaylord."

Elizabeth reacted as if she had received an electric shock. "You mean it was your husband who shot Gaylord?"

"Yes. You didn't know?"

Elizabeth vividly recalled the article. She had still been a hostage at Glenwood, but she remembered that the piece had made no mention of a suspect in the shooting, and once she had gotten away from the Center, she hadn't thought any more of the incident---- until now.

"At any rate, my husband left this suicide note." She removed a sheet of paper from the manila envelope. **IMPORTANT** was heavily stenciled across its face. "It is very personal, but as you will see from the section at the bottom that I've outlined in red, he directed me to this briefcase." Theresa Baxter handed Elizabeth the note.

Returning it after reading, Elizabeth asked. "Just what did the briefcase contain? This?" She indicated the orderly arrangement of documents on the edge of her desk. Theresa Baxter nodded somberly. "I hope you won't mind me asking," Elizabeth asked, "but why did your husband want to kill Gaylord?"

"This." Theresa Baxter indicated the contents of the briefcase. "And the fact that Gaylord is a hideous monster." She sighed impatiently. "Excuse me. I must not get emotional. You want the facts, right?"

"But I can understand your emotions because if you're right about Gaylord being the monster I suspect he is, then that monster is responsible for the deaths of my father and my best friend so I don't care how you convey the information. I just need to hear it."

Theresa Baxter seemed relieved. "I came to you because my husband wanted to do it himself. He just never got around to doing it. Anyway, just before everything happened, he called you but at the time he had the Senator on the other line. After his talk with the Senator, he abruptly disconnected you. He was visibly disturbed and left the room, but forgot to take your number. That's how I was able to contact your office."

"Why didn't you call sooner?"

"I did, but your secretary kept informing me that you were unavailable."

"Held hostage was more like it," Elizabeth whispered.

"For a while, I thought of doing nothing until I realized you were involved in the Safety Pins case and I saw the references to you in my husband's notes. Then I recognized that your life might be in danger because of Gaylord's intense hatred of you."

Elizabeth switched on a tape recorder. "Start wherever you want too, but please state your name for the record."

Almost as if she was talking to an invisible friend, Theresa Baxter closed her eyes as she spoke. "My name is Theresa Baxter and I have in my possession, documents that suggest that my husband, James Baxter, now deceased, along with Senator Junius Gaylord were involved in a conspiracy...." Her voice faltered. She looked bravely at Elizabeth and continued. "They were involved in a plot to imprison black men for profit."

Tears filled Elizabeth's eyes. At long last, she would have proof of her September 1st conspiracy theory. "Excuse me for crying," she pleaded, "but you just may be able to help me make sense out of the last few months of my life. It has been very, very strange to say the least." She dabbed at her eyes with the corners of her handkerchief. "Tell me about the conspiracy?"

"Do you, Miss Sellers, know what a puppet is?"

Elizabeth fumbled for a response.

"Would you like to see one?" Theresa Baxter reached inside a pocket of the briefcase and passed a photo across the desk. "That is a puppet."

"My God," Elizabeth shrieked. *"This is a photo of Vincent Taylor!"*

"He belonged to my husband."

"Belonged to your.....I don't understand."

"The Senator gave him to my husband."

"Gave him!" Elizabeth started. "What do you mean? How?"

"Part of the conspiracy was that one out of every four black boys was to go to prison. The unfortunate ones were to be chosen by some kind of lotto and then assigned to white men, such as my husband, who would then be responsible for manipulating their lives, controlling them, and most importantly leading them to prison like lambs going to slaughter."

Elizabeth was flabbergasted. "Puppets? Was...Is something like this even possible. I mean, control like that?" She shivered, thinking of William and Warren.

Evidently the Senator thought so and was able to convince the others involved that it was possible and from what I've read in my husband's diary, the Senator had every right to be optimistic."

Elizabeth was angry. "What are you saying? Who gave him such power?"

"His puppet, I imagine. From all accounts, the Senator was able to do with him as he pleased, and without the poor guy even suspecting a thing. Due to the Senator's meddling, the man has spent virtually all his life behind bars."

"Poor man," Elizabeth moaned. "I feel so sorry for him."

"The feeling will pass," Theresa Baxter said curtly. *"The puppet's name is Eugene Larry!"*

Elizabeth froze, unable to move, talk or think. Her mouth made inaudible sounds. Her well-manicured hands flopped aimlessly through the air, trying to coax words out into the open as though she was a maestro attempting to conduct music from an orchestra. Gradually, the terrifying numbness that had seized her dissolved into less constricting pressure, granting her the freedom to breathe normally once more. The darkness left the air. Oxygen returned. "Eugene Larry," she gasped. "So that's how he fits in."

"And in the end, the Senator turned him loose on you. Did you know that someone was out to get you?"

"Very much so," Elizabeth croaked. "Very much so."

"You must stop them," Theresa Baxter announced before leaving. "Or else."

After the Baxter woman had left, Elizabeth carefully studied the info on her desk and in the briefcase, and slowly the pieces of the puzzle slowly started to fall into place. One thing stood out most. Gaylord was a monster that had to be stopped. She grimaced. She would get the others involved as well. She wouldn't let any of them escape. She would see to it personally. But how? Most of the people involved were referred to by initials and on a lot of matters, James Baxter had only provided scratchy details, omitting vital incriminating information, but still she knew that it was much bigger than she or Lou had guessed.

A conspiracy against black men.

It was not quite nine that night when she left the office, tired and a little hungry. She wanted to call Lou immediately to report her findings, but decided to wait. She wanted to cleanse herself of this sordid ordeal as quickly as possible. She privately conceded that there could be no rest for her until she had seen this thing through. She had to destroy Ronpis, Gaylord's guide to eternal wealth. The ultimate get-rich-quick scheme.

Elizabeth got into her car.

Home.

The dark-skinned man had that feeling again. It had become familiar over the last two weeks. *He was not alone.* He removed the gun from under his pillow. He listened. Heard nothing. Listened some more. He got up slowly, gun in hand, safety off. He silently entered the kitchen, moving towards the back door, flowing soundlessly into the odd mixture of seeing nothing and yet knowing something was there--- somewhere.

Conditioned to be cautious, the man peered nervously over his shoulder. Once. Twice. Again. Then he tested the back door. It was locked. Moving swiftly out of the shadows, he took a single, looping, cross-over step in the direction of the pantry. It was to his left. From his immediate right, tight at his elbow, he sensed movement. In a single, fluid motion he thrust the gun behind the refrigerator, holding it steady. He squeezed the trigger. The bark of the gun was muffled, the bullet slamming into the wall. There was only emptiness behind the appliance. And now a hole.

Turning, he saw----no, he felt pain. A fat, beefy hand crashed into his skull, knocking him senseless. The gun clattered harmlessly to the floor.

"It's a good day for dying, my brotha," the big man spat, "but it ain't got to go down like that. I don't want the blood of another black man on my hands, but I won't think twice about killing you if it comes to that point."

"Wh-what is this all about?" Eugene Larry stammered.

The big man's companion, a medium-sized, brown-skinned man with a thick beard spoke. "We do not play games. That is something I want you to remember at all times." He nodded at the big man. The fat hand crashed into Eugene Larry's face with the power of a jackhammer. Eugene Larry spat out blood, a tooth, more blood. "That was just a wake-up call. Now, this is how we say Good Morning." The big men stood Eugene Larry up straight and the brown-skinned man with the shepherd's beard pummeled Eugene Larry's belly and kidneys with a succession of blows that bowled him over, doubling him in half. He was pushed back into a chair, huffing and puffing, gasping for air.

"Is there something you don't understand about the way we operate, brotha?"

Eugene Larry sagged in defeat. "If it's about her, man, I'm sorry. I didn't have no choice. You gotta believe me. You don't know the whole story."

The big man jacked Eugene Larry up again and shook him as if he was a stuffed doll. "If we didn't know the whole story," he growled, "you'd be dead by now." He slammed Eugene Larry down into the chair.

The brown-skinned man opened the refrigerator, extracted a bottle of grape juice. "This shit any good." He removed the cap, poured a third upon Eugene Larry's head. "It better be," he snarled viciously before slamming the empty bottle forcefully in the tiny opening between Eugene Larry's legs.

The bottle just missed crushing Eugene Larry's testicles. Eugene Larry screamed pitifully as mounds of sweat splayed his forehead and plied down the back of his neck. His asshole got hot. He swallowed, choking on panic.

"Like we said," the brown-skinned man intoned flatly, "if we didn't know what was up with you, we would have knocked your ass off a long time ago. We don't bullshit, but since we know you were coerced into doing that dumb shit to the sista, we gonna let you get a little get-back, some revenge, if you know what I mean."

"Y'all got me confused. Revenge? Get-back?"

"Don't play guessing games 'cause it's war and you can't straddle the fence. You either get down with your people or you roll with your cracker buddies. The choice is yours," the big man commented.

"Wh-what I gotta do?"

The brown-skinned man dropped a sheath of papers onto the kitchen table. "Read!"

Eugene Larry started to read the words.

Suddenly, Eugene Larry knew. It now was all crystal clear. He hadn't stood a chance. He broke down in tears, bawling like a whipped child, his blood boiling. His whole body quaked. He knew, understood that his life had been stolen, that he was not even considered human, but rather a toy.....a puppet. His entire existence had been scripted.

"You see what he has done?" Eugene Larry cried out. "You see what that motherfucka has done too me?" His words turned into sobs as the pain became almost unbearable. All he could do before crumbling into a broken heap upon the table was to gesture wildly with his hands as they punctuated the air, telling of his torment.

The two men left the room.

After about five minutes, Eugene Larry emerged from the kitchen, his face wrinkled from crying. He stood stiffly at the end of the living room sofa, staring vacantly. He felt tortured. "Whatever we do," he croaked, "save Gaylord for me."

The mood in the office was explosive and although he spoke in slow, controlled tones, Senator Gaylord was seething inside. "It is nothing," he said reassuring. "Nothing at all."

Dean Leroster was not so convinced. He even said as much. "I don't like this, Senator. Now that Eugene Larry------"

"*Puppet*," Gaylord corrected. "He is still under my command. *My puppet*," he grumbled selfishly.

"Whatever he is," Leroster protested testily, "he spells trouble. You of all people should know this. You heard what the nigger said. The tapes were fucking eloquent. Those jigs were not discussing the price of watermelons. They know, dammit, so they must die. The bitch too."

The Senator nodded in agreement. He flipped Leroster a key. "Jenners has the only other one. If the shit hits the fan, everything goes up in smoke and I mean every scrap of paper in the place. You got that?"

It was now Leroster's time to nod his head. He tucked the key away.

"Here's the address to the storage room." Senator Gaylord's voice turned dark. "If the shit hits the fan, everything goes up in smoke, remember?"

"Sure thing, boss."

"At this point, everything can be contained, but everyone who knows or may even be suspected of knowing must die."

"How soon?'

"Within the next forty eight hours tops. I have a list of names. You still got a tap on the phone?"

"Yeah, yeah," Leroster mumbled. "Everything is still in place. The joint is wired to the gills and the dumb cluck doesn't have a clue. Why don't you fly off somewhere for a week and by the time you get back to the States, this little stink of yours will be fixed."

"Thanks, but I think I'll stick around. I want a ringside seat for this one. Make that bitch beg and scream, will you?"

"My pleasure."

The words, although a weighty pair, seemed so inadequate.

"I'm sorry,' Eugene Larry told Elizabeth. "I really, really mean that."

There was not much time for anything else. They had a plane to catch. Elizabeth had at first experienced a terrible, gargantuan rage when she had first seen Eugene Larry. His black face, so close, so near, stirred her lingering anger to new and staggering heights. Her heart hardened. His presence seemed to invite further aggression against her and in her tired, weary eyes he was the embodiment of all the negative things that had happened too her. She thought of her father....Sandra....Glenwood....and so much more.

Lou was philosophical. "I know his saying that he's sorry is not much of an anesthesia, Miss Sellers, and I know the brotha is still agonizing inside over what he put you through, but y'all a team now, sista. Got to shake hands and keep it moving."

"Look," Qayyam interjected. "It's time to roll. Gotta catch that flight."

"Once you show Jenners the proof, I don't think you'll have any problems out of him. When he sees that the end is near, being a lawyer will make him scream for immunity and hand over the key to where the other files are." Lou seemed sure.

"What if he doesn't?" Elizabeth asked.

"Then I'll give him a good reason to change his mind." Eugene Larry smashed his right fist into the open palm of his left hand." Elizabeth shuddered.

Qayyam tapped a beefy finger in Eugene Larry's chest. "Take care of the sista, brotha. Since none of us are able to go with you, you better be on point until you can hook up with my peeps out there."

"The sista will be fine," Eugene Larry said sincerely. "I just hope she doesn't kill me."

A slight smile touched Elizabeth's lip. "Grab the bags, so we can go."

Lou handed Elizabeth a number. "As soon as you get the key and instructions from Jenners, call Laskey, an old buddy of mine who is with the feds. He said he could move on those clowns for civil rights violations."

"What about the murder of my dad?"

"They'll pay for that also. The civil rights violation is simply enough to hold them while the Justice

Department launches a real investigation into the whole Ronpis set-up."

"Wow," Eugene Larry exclaimed, "this shit is going to blow the public's mind."

"And," Qayyam added, "you two will be heroes."

"I just want my life back," Elizabeth retorted.

"Me," Eugene Larry stated blankly," I just want the Senator."

Off they went.

Jenners knew it. His old college chum and lifelong buddy had turned on him. The bastard hadn't even given him the benefit of the doubt. Just sicced the dogs on him with all deliberate speed and that was why he had agreed to meet Elizabeth Sellers. Their meeting would take place within the half hour.

The dame was onto them and if there was an easy way out, he was taking it. Hell, he was a lawyer. He wouldn't jump at the first deal. He wouldn't cower at the first signs of trouble unless the bitch really had his ass nailed to the cross. Then he would abandon ship as speedily as possible.

Even though his degree of involvement was not at all unusual from a legal standpoint, it was highly questionable in a number of other regards which underlined a very obvious fact: He was indictable. That was reason enough to start him drinking. One brandy snifter had led to another until he was no longer thinking coherently. That was the case until he had decided to drive home and had found his driveway filled with an assortment of strange vehicles. Instantly, he knew who they were and why they had come. Instantly, he was sober.

Damn Gaylord.

Now, he was branded. *A traitor.* Jenners shivered as he knew precisely what that
label meant: death!

The pickup truck handled rather clumsily, so unlike his Ferrari, but it was reliable and would get him there. He turned onto the freeway.

Only seconds after the pilot announced they were landing, both Elizabeth and Eugene Larry scurried from their seats and scrambled towards the bathroom. Eugene Larry went in first. Elizabeth waited at the door. The other passengers prepared to disembark.

Anxiety rising, Elizabeth waited a minute then tapped on the door. "You decent yet?"

"Almost. Gimme another second or two."

"Hurry up," Elizabeth chimed. "People from first class are getting off."

The climate of anticipation was too much for Elizabeth. She rapped on the door again. "Now?" she asked.

"Yes, now. Come on in."

As important as the moment was, Elizabeth could not suppress the laughter. It rolled out of her mouth involuntarily. She stuffed her knuckle into her mouth and clamped down on it to diffuse the comic import of the image she saw.

"You sure don't have to worry about being hit on. Look at that wig," she sighed. "Hand me that blush. Putting on makeup is not like painting a fence. Now, stand still."

Eugene Larry closed his eyes and could feel Elizabeth's fingers gently at work on his face, only vaguely aware of the makeup's dramatic ability to transform. Elizabeth lavished her skills upon him, filling in, downplaying, and coloring his masculine features until they were deceptively influenced by a femininity that vibrated.

Elizabeth reached into her carrying bag and pulled out a long, black chador, the flowing garb that Muslim women from Iran wore. She slipped it over her head and it fell down over the full length of her body, completely covering her sweater and jeans. She applied kohl to her eyes, darkening them and then pulled the veil over her face until only the eyes were visible.

They stared at each other. At least now, they were no longer sitting ducks. They squeezed out of the bathroom. Elizabeth first. Then Eugene Larry. Outside on the long concourse, Eugene Larry fell in silent step beside the Muslim-garbed Elizabeth.

"You still look like a cheap floozy," Elizabeth whispered out of the side of her mouth.

"Is that good or bad?"

"And please don't talk. Just give the cab-driver the address. "You no speak English, okay?" They neared the top of the concourse. "Once you get into the terminal, you're on your own. Just get behind a woman and watch her walk. Then you do it like she does."

"Does what?"

"Walk."

"Okay."

"Goodbye."

As expected, people were busy going every which way inside the airport, merging in and out of the various concourses, flowing easily from one level to another. Elizabeth stood stiffly, watching Eugene Larry walk. It could still use some improvement, but it was much too late for that now. Suddenly, he was lost in the crowd, swallowed up by the color and pageantry of everyday people doing normal things, but somewhere out here, she knew were some not-so-everyday people. They were professional killers. And they were out to get her. And the Ace-of-Spades "Woman."

Elizabeth meshed into the oases of moving bodies and surged towards the exit. Under her disguise, her blood boiled as if a bubbling cauldron. At this juncture in what lied ahead, she had to be sure she wanted to press on because death could be just around the corner.

At the exit door, she made up her mind and walked out into the California sunshine. She hailed a taxi. A little further up the block, Eugene Larry did the same. They both were still alive. So far. So good.

Twenty minutes later, both cabs stopped at a crowed park where a free open concert was in full bloom. On center stage, a posse of wannabe gangsta rappers were loudly dissing homeboys across the bay. Elizabeth didn't expect to find Jenners at his venue. She heard jazz and moved in that direction.

Elizabeth glanced around, Eugene Larry following somewhat back, but close enough. She felt out of place. Her garb and the atmosphere seemed contradictory. She looked for Jenners. *Suppose he had gotten chicken?* He knew exactly what time they were due to meet so he should have been standing near the main entrance. She almost mumbled a curse, but remembered her disguise and prayed instead. Her walking prayer didn't last long as she soon spotted Jenners standing nervously in front of a hot-dog vendor. She slowed down so that Eugene Larry could catch up.

"There he is," she said. "White shirt. Coat slung over his shoulder."

"Let's not approach him yet," Eugene Larry suggested. "Let's see if he's with someone or if anybody is watching him."

For a little over ten minutes, Jenners stood there unmoving except for an anxious two steps to his right, two steps to his left and then back to his original spot.

He was apparently alone. *Unwatched?* Well, that was anyone's guess.

They approached cautiously.

"Jenners!"

At the mention of his name, Jenners jumped, staring at the black-clad figure.

"It's me, Elizabeth Sellers." She paused. "I quite sure you recognize my voice."

"Damn," Jenners exclaimed, "and I thought I was playing it safe. What now?"

"We talk."

"Where?"

"Inside the crowd," Eugene Larry cracked.

Jenners jumped again.

"He's with me," Elizabeth commented matter-of-factly.

"He?"

"It's a long story," Elizabeth confessed.

The three of them pushed their way into the crowd surrounding the bandstand. People were grooving, clapping, feeling good as they celebrated the smooth jazz. The trio talked. In the midst of all this commotion, they found a way to communicate and at the end of ten minutes, they were all on the same page. They were a team. For better...or for worse.

Or death would do them part.

They knew where Jenners would go.

Pressing their advantage, Leroster lined the highway with hired killers and waited. *Jenners had to come this way.* It would then be a race to see who would get to the storage warehouse first. Whoever did, got the papers.

When the word came in some ten minutes later that Jenners had been spotted, Leroster grunted with pleasure at this mixed blessing. At least, now they knew where Jenners was, where he was going, but he was ahead of them in the race to get to where the Senator's papers were. Since it was evident they couldn't outrun him, they now simply had to outgun him. That should be fairly easy.

Speeding through the small, sleepy town, Jenners clearly perceived the desperate consequences. It would come down to a defiant battle of life and death as he realized they were pitted against callous men intent on preserving the sanctity of their guilt. The idea of compromise, of effecting a truce was laughable. He understood his options. Clearly.

"Look behind the seat," Jenners hollered at Eugene Larry. "Hope you know how to use one of those things."

"In all the movies I've ever seen, they always just pulled the trigger and the gun did the rest."

"That's the general idea. They're fully automatic and loaded." Jenners peered into the rearview mirror. "And ready."

Four minutes later, a nondescript Chevy tried to ramrod Jenners's truck as it sped past a lonely intersection. The truck hit in the tail, skidded in a tight arc, propelling the vehicle into a forced spin. Jenners applied the brakes, keeping the nose of the truck out of a lateral roll as the Chevy came up again, hitting the back fender. Jenners lurched forward, his chest smashing against the steering wheel.

The impact flung Elizabeth into the dash of the truck, her head crashing brutally into the pane. Blood gushed from a cut above her eye. She did not move.

"*Oh my God,*" Eugene Larry groaned. "*Elizabeth!*"

"For Christ's sake, man,' Jenners bellowed as the car rammed them a third time, "what are you waiting for. *Shoot!*" He slid open the small window behind the seat. "If you don't, they sure as hell will."

Eugene Larry stared at the slumped over figure of Elizabeth and spun around, placing his knees on the seat. He steadied the assault rifle on the ledge of the window.

"*Shoot!*" Jenners yelled. "Don't take aim. *Just shoot!*"

The sounds of rapid gunfire exploded in the cabin of the truck as Eugene Larry peppered the Chevy with bullets. The vehicle fell back.

"Thank God," Jenners croaked.

"I think I got one,' Eugene Larry offered vacantly. "I saw...."

"No time for tears," Jenners cracked. "Better check on Miss Sellers. We're almost there."

"Look out!"

From out of the density of the trees on both sides of the road, two cars zoomed out of hiding. They jetted into Jenners' path, forming a barricade as the drivers leaped from the vehicles, aiming weapons.

Eugene Larry didn't have to be told this time. He rammed the rifle through the window and squeezed off a tremendous burst of fire, sweeping to the left, mowing down one of the men. To his right, the other man tried to flee, but the bullets that followed in his wake, found him, tearing a huge chunk of flesh from the back of his head and shoulders.

Jenners plowed the truck through the barricade as though the cars were a spider's web.

Elizabeth stirred.

"How much farther?" Eugene Larry asked.

"A few more miles, but I don't think we should go there."

"Why?" Elizabeth moaned weakly.

"They're probably there waiting for us."

"But we've come all this way," she protested.

"And not just to die, I hope," Jenners remarked hotly. He thought for a second. "There's a store up ahead."

Then it dawned on Elizabeth. "I forgot to call Laskey."

"Who?"

"He's help," Elizabeth chortled.

Jenners grunted. "Let's hope this friend of yours has the speed of Superman because time is not on our side. Be sure to let Laskey know this."

After a brief phone conversation, Elizabeth sighed. "I told him where we were headed and he said he'd put some men on it."

Jenners glared at Elizabeth. "What a fine mess. We can't stay here because in about three minutes, this place is going to be crawling with killers, and we can't go to the warehouse without help. If you trust your people, then our lives are in their hands."

"We're going in?" Eugene Larry quizzed.

"Not much choice, actually," Jenners admitted. "The only way we can survive this now is to snatch those papers before they do and get them in the lap of federal authorities, but we have no time to waste. I don't have the only key to the warehouse and more than likely Gaylord or someone is trying to beat us there."

"If they get there before us---"

"We're doomed."

They tore out of the parking lot, Eugene Larry raking the distance with gunfire. He struck a tire. The car hissed air, then went flat. However, before the sensation of getting lucky could set in, another car zoomed down the road coming fast towards them. Eugene Larry poked the gun out of the window, finger tightening on the trigger, squeezing----"

"Don't shoot," Jenners yelled. "It's a woman with children in the back."

The burgundy Ford sped past.

"Whew," Eugene Larry rasped. "That was close."

"Well, don't relax. She's not driving that fast for nothing. Whatever it is that spooked her probably means bad news for us." Abruptly, he smashed on the brakes. Skidding, the truck halted. "You drive," he told Elizabeth. "I'm getting in the back. Two shooters are better than one. We're getting ready to drive into hell. May God bless us."

The truck lurched forward.

About two hundred yards from the warehouse sign, the street once deserted, became crammed with cars. Immediate gunfire erupted over the hood of the truck, sending men howling and screaming, running for cover. The gunfire was returned. Elizabeth did her best to keep the truck steady as she ducked her head down under the dash. The entire front window shattered, splashing splinters of glass down upon her. She yelped as she felt shards of glass on her neck.

Bullets pelted the truck.

"OWWW!" Jenners was hit.

"Oh my God," Elizabeth cried out as she heard Jenners fall back onto the bed of the truck."He's dead," she shrieked.

Eugene Larry raised up, pumping bullets out of the front of the truck. By now, Jenners had pulled himself back up. He was bleeding badly, but still alive.

"Floor this bastard," Jenners cursed, "and go right through the fucking gate."

CRASH!

Once inside the perimeter.

"Straight down, then left at H," Jenners commanded. "It's bin 38." He passed a key to Elizabeth. "Pull the truck in front of the door. We'll cover you."

Within seconds, even though her hands trembled, she was in.

"Close the door and don't come out until I tell you too."

"Here they come," Eugene Larry yelled, sending a short, quick burst of bullets at the approaching cars.

A bullet smashed through the aluminum door, chipping metal from off the file cabinet. Elizabeth screamed. Another bullet buried itself into the wall over her head. Then some more whizzed through, tattooing and riddling the interior of the storage bin. Elizabeth screamed again, covering her head. She pulled the file cabinet away from the wall and crouched down behind it. She feared for her life.

She heard someone howl out in pain. Jenners? Eugene Larry? One of the two had been hit. Then a brief eerie, numbing silence. Then an agonizing shout. Then a furious round of shooting. Another howl of pain. Another. Still another.

Then one more.

After about ten minutes of horrifying quiet, footsteps. Many of them. At the door. Stopped. Elizabeth's breath caught in her throat as she heard voices, listened to them.

"They're dead," one of the voices intoned solemnly. "Both of them."

"Where's the woman?"

"Probably dead too."

A frantic ten seconds elapsed before Elizabeth heard the grating sound of the door being lifted. She watched in terror as it rose higher, lifting up, making room for the men to enter. She would be brave, would not beg. Would not be a coward. Everyone before her....Sandra...her father...Jenners....Eugene Larry had all died heroically. No whining. Well she was the last one left and she was determined to do the same. She rose to her full height as ice ran cold in her veins. She faced the men, her voice strong.

"My name is Elizabeth Sellers." She thrust out her chin defiantly. "Let's get this over with.'

"My name," the man replied, "is Bernard Littlejohn, FBI. Laskey sent me."

A huge wave of relief flooded over Elizabeth, She felt ready to start shouting. "God is the greatest," she proclaimed. "It's all over. I won."

Then she cried.

"Slavery has been fruitful in giving itself names. It has been called "The Peculiar Institution," The Social System," and "The Impediment". It has been called by a great many names, and it will call itself by yet another name, and you and I and all of us better wait and see what new term this old monster will assume, in what new skin this old snake will come forth next."
-Frederick Douglass

If, by chance, you enjoyed this book, then please check out my other books at <u>www.soulfirebooks.com</u>